THE 40 DAYS
A NOVEL

A story about Jesus Christ and the days
before He returned to Heaven—the days
not recorded in the Bible. Grow in faith
and believe in the grace of God; learn the
meaning of being a Christian, and why
there is hope for tomorrow.

F . B . TIMMERMAN

CARDAMOM PUBLISHERS
JANESVILLE, WI

The 40 Days: A Novel. A Story about Jesus Christ and the days before He returned to Heaven—the days not recorded in the Bible. Grow in faith and believe in the grace of God; learn the meaning of being a Christian, and why there is hope for tomorrow.

Published by
Cardamom Publishers
P.O. Box 2146
Janesville, WI 53547

Printed in the United States of America

ISBN 978-0-9742181-8-2
Library of Congress Control Number: 2011927112
Library of Congress Subject Heading: 1. Christian fiction.
2. Christian life – Biblical teaching. 3. Faith and reason - Christianity.

Cover illustration: Copyright © 2011 Cardamom Publishers
Back cover: Jerusalem from the south April 12th 1839,
David Roberts

DEDICATION

to my wonderful wife
and children.

Because you have seen me, you have believed; blessed are those who have not seen and yet have believed.

John 20:29 (NIV)

Not a Christian because of what Christians do –
but because of what Christ did.

CONTENTS

Preface vii

Prologue 1

Khirbet el-Maqatir
Discovery. 3
Dr. Naveh 10

Shemaiah's Story
Nisan 14 – Darkness . 13
Nisan 16 – Day 1 17
Day 2 – Pierced 21
Day 3 – Plans 28
Day 4 – Trust 32
Day 5 – The Word 33
Day 6 – Foretold 37
Day 8 – Sharing 43
Day 9 – Fearless 50
Day 11 – Pride 57
Day 12 – Envy 67
Day 13 – Children . . . 69
Day 15 – Divine 74
Day 16 – Forgive 82
Day 18 – As a Child . 87

Day 20 – Rules 91
Day 22 – Saved 96
Day 24 – Peace 100
Day 25 – Success . . . 108
Day 27 – Worship . . 117
Day 29 – Death 122
Day 32 – Heaven 135
Day 33 – Privilege . 142
Day 34 – Love 147
Day 38 – Servant . . . 152
Day 39 – Jars 156
Day 40 – Home 161

A New Beginning 165

References 173

Preface

You may know the stories of the Bible and believe that it's the inspired word of God. You may go to a church on Sunday and listen to the pastor's sermons and listen to the Holy Scriptures while they're being read. You may even read the Bible on the other days of the week. Or perhaps you go through the motions on Sunday and then go on with your life the rest of the week.

Whatever your situation, do you truly believe that what you hear is true, or are you just afraid to believe it isn't true?

Do you pray looking for answers or help, don't sense that you get answers and wonder if God is listening?

Are you one of the many who have just never taken the time to find out what that 'Christian thing' is all about? Are you too busy to take the time?

Do you drive past churches that look like corporate headquarters and decide that the corporation you go to every day is already enough?

Have you tried reading the Bible to find out what it's about, but you don't understand what it says and then you lose interest?

Do you look at people and see different class levels and decide that believing in God isn't necessary in this high-tech age? You see that one group consists of successful business leaders, the politically powerful, the rich, the prestigious, the glamorous, the manipulators of money, and assume they all seem to be doing well and enjoying themselves. The other group consists of all the people that aren't in the first group—and you decide you want to be in the first group, the successful one. They don't seem to be accountable to some invisible power and they appear to be doing very well on their own.

Do you know people who call themselves Christians but act just the same as people who aren't, so you don't take their faith seriously?

Do you know people who call themselves Christians but act so differently from everyone else that you don't take them seriously?

Are you skeptical of the existence of a God and the belief that his Son—a person called Jesus—actually walked on this earth?

Do you think the old stories about Jesus are just that— old stories—but nothing more. If you had more proof maybe you would believe.

Do you even know who Jesus is?

If you don't know anything about Jesus or not enough to know how or if he should influence your life, maybe the following story will give you some insight and then arouse your curiosity to learn more.

If you do know Jesus, I hope this story will strengthen your faith and make you consider more fully how you would live your life if you had no doubts about the existence of Jesus; God and creator of the universe.

If you had one more bit of proof, something that removed all doubts about Jesus and acknowledged the love God has for all people, would that belief cause you to live your life differently, without so much worry, and with more compassion for others? What security you would have knowing that God has promised to watch over you and provide for you. On top of that, you'd be certain that death is not the end, but that through His Son, it's only the portal to a better and everlasting life.

That extra proof already exists—you only need to open your eyes and your heart to it.

Though this is a fictional story, I've tried to the best of my ability to reflect the Bible, and have added many endnotes that reference places in the Bible where the various topics can be found, many with Jesus' own words.

I hope this story helps you realize that Jesus represents God's love for people, encourages you to have a passion for learning more about Jesus, the Son of God, and helps you see that Jesus truly did exist, still exists, and will always exist.

And did I say it yet? The Bible doesn't say where Jesus was those last 40 days before he ascended into Heaven.

THE 40 DAYS

A NOVEL

.

Prologue

An archaeological discovery is always an exciting experience, but a discovery from Biblical times, especially the first
century, when the events recorded in the New Testament
took place, is especially exhilarating. Such is the discovery
that occurred after the recent torrential rains just north of
Jerusalem, between el-Bireh and et-Tell, at Khirbet el-
Maqatir.*

Khirbet el-Maqatir, just southwest of et-Tell, had become
more interesting to archaeologists as they found evidence
that the ancient city of Ai was located there and not at et-
Tell. The city of Ai is mentioned many times throughout the
Old Testament. Ai was the city that Joshua attacked after
Jericho had been conquered. To defeat Ai, Joshua split his
army: he chose 30,000 men to lie in ambush west of the city
while he and the rest of his forces drew out Ai's armies to the
north. The plan worked, as the Lord had directed Joshua,
and this city too was defeated by the army of Israel.

Beitin, a town northwest of et-Tell, was long thought to
have been the ancient city of Bethel. But recent analysis had
cast doubt on this location also. Archaeologists now believed
that el-Bireh, southwest of Beitin, was more likely to have
been the forgotten city of Bethel. After the Lord directed
Abraham (called Abram at that time) to:

---

* Khirbet el-Maqatir is pronounced (Ker-Bit el-Muh-Kah-ter)

> *"Leave your country, your people and your father's household and go to the land I will show you."* Genesis 12:1 (NIV)

Abram crossed this area:

> *"he went on toward the hills east of Bethel and pitched his tent, with Bethel on the west and Ai on the east. There he built an altar to the LORD and called on the name of the LORD." Genesis 12:8 (NIV)*

Now before the time of Joshua, but after Abraham, Jacob had also traveled this area. In fact, he spent the night there. While he slept, he had a dream:

> *in which he saw a stairway resting on the earth, with its top reaching to heaven, and the angels of God were ascending and descending on it. Genesis 28:12 (NIV)*

Much later, Jesus mentioned a similar scene when he was talking to Nathanael:

> *He then added, "I tell you the truth, you shall see heaven open, and the angels of God ascending and descending on the Son of Man." John 1:51 (NIV)*

Khirbet el-Maqatir

Discovery

The rain created pools of water that interrupted the archaeological dig at Khirbet el-Maqatir, Israel, so Ilan and his daughter Anna climbed up the neighboring hills to pass the time and enjoy the now-sunny weather and the distant views. Civilization had avoided the hills due to the rocky terrain. Over the rise were valleys and hills that shepherds had traversed with their flocks of sheep for centuries.

Ilan was only a part-time archaeologist. Archaeology was mainly a way for him to spend time with his daughter at times throughout the year. Anna had always been interested in history, poring through annals and biographies even when she was little. As a teenager she began to focus her interest toward archaeology and then went on to the Hebrew University of Jerusalem and received a B.A. (and later an M.A.) from the Department of Biblical Archaeology. At 33, she was very well respected in her field.

Ilan and Anna were heading southward, enjoying their conversation. Long ago, this land was described as flowing with milk and honey, and these hills were good for pasture and filled with plants and flowers. But after several miles, climbing the hills proved to be a little strenuous. The stroll through the rough terrain was now becoming a workout; the bright sun cast dark shadows, making it hard to see how to achieve secure footing when climbing. Ilan was more agile, so he thought, and advanced up the hill ahead of Anna.

"Maybe we'll find the ladder," he yelled.

"Ladder? What ladder?"

"Jacob's ladder. Well, not his personally, but the ladder he saw—you remember—in Genesis. You do remember something from your Hebrew classes, don't you?"

"Oh, *that* ladder," she replied.

But as Ilan turned to talk to Anna, he placed his foot on a rock. The recent rains had loosened the soil around the rock, and his weight caused it to slide and then flip out away from his foot. As the rock left its home, Ilan's foot took its place and then some.

The rock had concealed a hole, and now Ilan's leg plunged up to his knee in a crevice. He let out a yell, not so much in pain but from being startled, and in anticipation of what injury might occur. At first he thought his foot was stuck when he tried to pull it out of the hole, as his boot had slipped into an opening at the bottom of the crevice. With a little twisting, he pulled it out. Fortunately he was unscathed, except for a few scratches and a jolt to his body from quickly sitting down on rocks. Anna soon caught up with him and, seeing that her dad was alright, helped him to his feet.

As Ilan stood up, loose gravel fell into the hole. But when the gravel made a sound of landing after falling a distance, they both spun around and stared at the opening between the rocks. Anna's professional instincts took over and she began to investigate this opening in the rocks. She hastily removed her flashlight from her backpack and shined it into the hole. She realized immediately that this wasn't something that rain had washed away or that a pile of rocks had formed. This was something that had been made for a purpose.

Using their picks and small shovels (tools the archaeologist is never without), they pulled back rocks and gravel and soon opened the crevice to discover a hole or small pocket in the rocks. Peering in, they saw two clay pots with lids.

With mouths hanging open, Ilan and Anna stared in disbelief. Were the shadows playing tricks on them? Was this a hallucination? Anna removed her sunglasses and stuck her head further into the hole. Then she reached and touched the clay pot just to confirm what her eyes had seen. Anna and Ilan then pulled more rocks away from the opening, and Anna climbed in. She felt carefully around the nearest jar to make sure it was intact and then did the same to the second jar. Both appeared to be in excellent condition. She had always dreamed about unearthing something significant; every archaeologist dreamed this but very few uncovered the prize.

Ilan was overjoyed and, with hugs, complimented Anna on her discovery. This was his first experience with a real find. His involvement in digs had never produced much: just a few odds and ends that were usually just broken portions of a larger piece, the rest having disappeared long ago.

Anna was excited as well, but her analytical mind was already at work. She tried to place these pots in their proper place in time: these pots were very unique. But at the same time Anna thought they looked very familiar, and then it came to her. These clay pots were almost identical to those found in the caves at Khirbet Qumran. Those vessels contained what became known as the Dead Sea Scrolls, some of the oldest existing Old Testament documents, dating from 150 BC to 70 AD. They predated anything previous by nearly a thousand years.

The pots they were admiring were in excellent condition; they had been placed in a raised corner and protected from above by a ledge. Any water would have drained away from the treasure. The pots appeared whole, covered only in a layer of sandy dust.

Anna tried to lift the lid but time had sealed it tight, and that was a good thing. If something was actually inside the jar, then there was a better chance that it was intact. She tried to rock the clay pot. With a little effort, it started to move. She scraped away at the base and soon the jar was free. Her heart raced at this incredible discovery. Ilan stayed out of the way, but his huge smile showed how proud he was of Anna, and how happy he was to be there to share the experience.

Anna wanted to remove the lids from the jars and continue the discovery but professional discipline controlled her. She took out her phone, called the director and asked for assistance in order to do the uncovering properly.

Hours later, the jars were removed from the hole, carefully transported down the hill and taken back to Khirbet el-Maqatir, where the dig's storage building was located. Anna and Ilan placed the jars on large wooden tables and secured them to prevent them from tipping over. Keeping them in the same position as they had been for centuries was the safest way to preserve them. Ilan sat on a tall stool against the wall and out of the way while Anna and her colleagues processed the vessels. There were people in the room now whom Ilan had never seen at Khirbet el-Maqatir. He assumed they were from Hebrew University, and he wondered how they had arrived so quickly.

The clay pots were examined slowly and deliberately. Photographs were taken with digital cameras, measurements made at all levels, the pots were slowly cleaned and the dislodged sand was collected and bagged. During the process, the suspense built until Ilan wanted to rush to the table and lift the lids himself, but he took a deep breath and settled back down on the stool.

Eventually it was decided that it was time. The lids should come off; further examination of the clay pots could be made later. But as they began concentrating on loosening the lid, they stopped. Ilan could see the examiners pointing at something and then dusting and blowing the dirt away. Then they approached the other jar and it was slowly turned around and examined closer. Eye loupes were pressed against eyes and each person around the table took a close look at the clay pots, at a point just below each lid.

Ilan caught Anna's attention and silently mouthed, "What's going on?"

Anna replied, "Alpha and Omega," and then repeated "Alpha and Omega."

"What does that mean?" Ilan asked.

Anna held her hands out palm-side up and shrugged, then smiled and pointed up.

The chatter quieted down. It was once again time to remove the lid. Anna was given the honor of removing the lid from the first treasure since she had made the discovery. The seal had already been cleaned, so only a few taps on the lid were required and then it moved, causing Anna to jump a little. With gloved hands, she removed the lid, and a slight gasp could be heard in the quiet room. All eyes were on the clay pot, but no one said a word.

Anna handed the lid off, reached into the vessel and pulled out a magnificent scroll wrapped in fine linen. Exclamations abounded in different languages. Anna held the scroll high and turned around so all could see. Then she carefully laid the scroll on a nearby clean table.

Attention now turned to the second vessel. The honor of opening this vessel had been given to Dr. Amnon Naveh, a popular former professor at the university and easily the oldest person in the room. With shaking hands, Dr. Naveh tapped the lid loose and found another scroll. Dr. Naveh removed the scroll from the second clay pot but had to be steadied by two people as his legs started to buckle from the excitement. This scroll was placed on a different clean table.

The linen was carefully pulled back in order to examine the scrolls. Initial examination by those present thought the scrolls to be made of sheepskin, probably from the first century, but that would be determined later. But there were features that nobody recognized. These were very unique scrolls. A quick test was made to see if it would be possible to unroll the scrolls: that, too, was successful. The scrolls were then placed in sealed boxes and it became obvious that the event was coming to a close.

Ilan was confused by what was happening. He motioned for Anna. Anna walked over to her father, feeling as though she was gliding on air from the exhilaration of the discovery. She told Ilan that the next step would be a delicate process carried out by experts. The scrolls would be carefully unrolled and photographed. The condition of the scrolls would determine the speed of the progress in reading the contents.

Arrangements were made to celebrate the day's events at a restaurant in Ramallah. Anna and her father joined in the festivities and were the recipients of many toasts. The celebration went on for many hours until Ilan, himself tired from the long day, noticed that Anna was deep in thoughts far removed from the party and convinced her that it was time to leave.

Anna's thoughts were indeed not at the party, as she was trying to resolve the meaning of the scrolls. Reflecting on the opinions expressed today, Anna couldn't agree with her colleagues and others from the university who felt that since these scrolls probably weren't as old as the Dead Sea Scrolls, they likely duplicated information they already had. They felt that it was a great discovery, but not one that would rewrite, or even get mentioned in, archaeological journals. But Anna wasn't convinced. Most of those in the room today were Jewish, but she was different. She was born again: a believer in Jesus.

The pools of water receded, and Anna and Ilan were able to get in a few days together at the dig site. There was no new excitement and time passed uneventfully. It was a typical dig for an archaeologist. From a distance, they were able to observe a small distinguished group enter and exit the storage building every day, led by Dr. Naveh, but there was no word on their findings.

So at the end of the week, Ilan went back to his wife, Ronia, in Jerusalem, and then back to work for Bezeq, the telephone company, in the billing department. Meanwhile, Anna continued her work at Khirbet el-Maqatir.

D r .   N a v e h

Four weeks later, Ronia called Ilan to the phone. "You're daughter is 'over the moon' about something. You'd better talk to her."

It was all Anna could do to control her excitement and explain that Dr. Naveh had just called her about the scrolls.

"He's never seen anything like this before—never imagined anything like this was possible—the scrolls were in incredible condition and easily translated since they were written in classic Hebrew!"

Anna paused for a breath and composed herself.

"Since Dr. Naveh led the examination of the scrolls this past month, he decided that we should be the first to be presented with the findings. He wants us there at 9:00 tomorrow morning."

"Tomorrow is very soon."

"I know, but Dr. Naveh said the content is very significant," Anna replied.

"Where does he want us to go?" Ilan asked.

"Here, at Khirbet el-Maqatir."

"Well, I work tomorrow but I'll figure something out. Can I bring your mother?"

"Yes, and I've already asked her."

"Then we'll see you in the morning."

Morning came and Ilan, Ronia and Anna were ushered into the storage building along with a few of Dr. Naveh's assistants and colleagues from the Hebrew University. Chairs surrounded the large wooden table that again held the first clay jar. Dr. Naveh sat at the side of the table: the clay jar was on his left, Anna and her parents sat across from him, and the others sat in various other places to his right. A binder containing a stack of papers, some glasses, and a pitcher of water were in front of him.

The sun shone brightly through the east windows, trying to heat the room. Wind blowing in through open windows could cause damage to the artifacts inside, so the windows were kept closed and the air conditioner was already running. The hum of the generator outside the building was audible through the walls.

Dr. Naveh poured water into a glass, took a sip and then began.

"Thank you for coming here on such short notice. These scrolls..."

Dr. Naveh suddenly paused. His smile faded and he became very serious.

"...these scrolls have provided information that no one could have imagined. They will cause you to delve into your deepest soul, to undergo a personal deliberation or rumination into what you have been taught and what you have believed since your youngest days. You will walk away from here changed, because that *is* the purpose of these scrolls."

The three guests shifted in their chairs. Their hearts beat a little faster. The room got a little bit warmer. They unconsciously reached out and held each others' hands. Ilan glanced at the door as if an escape might be needed.

Dr. Naveh's smile returned.

"But don't be afraid. I hope you will find this message enlightening."

He adjusted his glasses, and then looked at Anna and her parents.

"Are you ready?" he asked.

Ilan, Ronia and Anna slowly nodded yes, and Dr. Naveh picked up the first sheet and began to read aloud.

Shemaiah's Story

Nisan 14 – Darkness

This record of events is from Shemaiah, a shepherd from the hills north of Beth-Basi, the husband of Meira and the father of Daniel, the son of Nathan, whose wife was Margalit, who named me "he who hears the Lord."

During the time of Herod Antipas and Pilate, the governor in Jerusalem, and at the time of the Passover celebration, I was tending my sheep in the hills. In searching for fertile fields, I had led my flock of 94 sheep north of our home. We had even gone beyond Bethany. Many years of clearing brush and careful work had provided fertile fields to go for grazing.

This season I was reluctant to travel far, for Meira was ill, but her sister was nearby and assured us that she would care for her. But I was still concerned. Because of her illness, my son came with me. He is a helper for me but an extra concern as well. He is strong, but he was born slow of mind and speech. He is dearly loved and near manhood but he will always be a child. God has blessed us with his gentle and pleasant spirit.

God also blessed us by providing favorable weather for the start of our journey. However, that changed four days ago on the day before the special Sabbath, which is also Passover.

We were in the fields at midday when the sky became very dark; the sun was not to be seen. This was not like other storms, for I have seen many. This was even darker, as if it was night.

The sheep became very nervous, stirring in all directions. Daniel was also afraid, for he does not like rough weather. We tried to protect the flock by moving them along the steeper hillsides, sheltering them away from the lightning and the crash of thunder. Even though the skies were dark, very dark, and the wind was having its way, it never did rain. But as the afternoon wore on, the heavens became more frightening. I could no longer provide assurance for the flock and they began to scatter.

By now I was working alone, for Daniel was also terrified. All I could do was try to limit the number of directions the sheep ran, instead of letting them go in all directions. We were moving, as I now know, in a northerly course, for at the time all references had become obscured.

The storm continued into the afternoon. When it seemed that the turmoil would never end, or that it couldn't get any worse, the ground began to shake, which terrified us even more. We did our best to move away from the tall hills as rocks began to fall. By the grace of God we weren't killed, since we were not able to escape to a protected shelter because the trembling earth brought us to our knees. Even the clouds appeared to be trembling as they twisted and turned in all directions, unlike anything I had ever seen before.

Eventually the rumbling stopped and the sky began to slowly lighten, though it remained dark gray in color. The wind and thunder ceased. It was as if some great powerful struggle in the heavens had ended, but who the victor was, I did not know.

I consoled my frightened son. We then began up righting the sheep that had fallen, at least those sheep that remained

in sight, for I now saw only one in three of the flock with
which I had begun my journey.

I started down the path the sheep had fled, proceeding at
a brisk pace. I looked back and forth quickly for any signs of
my flock but I wasn't very successful. My pursuit continued
into the evening, when darkness made it more difficult to
see. I tried to be careful of where I stepped, but often my
search took me awfully close to the edge of the rocks.

The cool night air caused some of the rocks to attract
moisture. I knew I must be extra cautious. But in the blink of
an eye, my sandal skidded on some damp mud on a rock and
I slipped and fell. I was falling over the ledge to certain injury—possibly even death—and then, as I reached out to
grab hold of *anything*, I felt hands grab my wrists and fore-
arms, stopping my fall, and even pulling my body up.

When I had a foothold for my feet, I looked upwards
and found that my left wrist was wrapped around some
vines. I pulled myself back up and unwrapped the vines. To
my amazement, this revealed the strangest sight: on my arms
were handprints and images of fingers, but they weren't
bruises. They were handprints and fingerprints that glowed.

With the knowledge I have now, I realize that God's
hand or that of an angel had seized me, saving me from im-
minent peril. I remember hearing how Moses, after being in
God's presence, had brought fear to the Israelites because his
face was radiant.[1] But at the time, my mind wasn't able to
come to that conclusion. I was just confused, so I got up and
continued fulfilling my responsibility to protect my flock.

I persisted in my search for the sheep. Sometimes I
would see one down an unlikely path. At other times, I
would hear a voice mixed in with the wind, not distinct but
more melodic, which caused me to turn and look in a certain
direction, and there I would see another one of my ewes. At

first I credited the noise to the baaing of the sheep. But after it happened a few times, I began to question myself, wondering if I was just hearing the wind playing tricks and causing sounds to echo among the rocks. I tried to recall if I might have hit my head when I fell and thus didn't have full control of my senses.

It became apparent to me that I wouldn't be able to unite the flock this night. With a calm voice, I worked to steady the sheep of my flock that remained. I would have to wait to pursue the deserters. I needed to allow our trembling souls to recover—mine, Daniel's and the sheep's—for this mysterious event had been very unnerving. Retrieving the lost would take considerable time. I prayed to the One who watches over us all to watch and protect these sheep as well.

The next day, Nisan 15, and also the high Sabbath, was spent in reflection, prayer and tending to my meager flock. The sky continued to be gray in color. I looked forward to tomorrow for it would be a new day, a new start, a new beginning for my journey.

Nisan 16 – Day 1

A new beginning it would prove to be. Very early in the morning, before the sun had arisen, I awoke suddenly to a slight rumble. At first I thought the strange storm was returning. But the rumble only occurred once, and I decided that it must have been some disturbance in distant Jerusalem. Now the heavens above were in bright splendor; it was a beautiful day for the Festival of First Fruits. No threatening clouds were visible in any direction, and from my position in the hills I could see for great distances.

After our morning prayers, Daniel and I gathered our cloaks (on which we had slept), our bags with provisions, and our shepherd's rods and staffs, and headed out in search for our sheep.

Our pace was slow and not very successful. As we herded the sheep, Daniel and I would search behind bushes and brush, up and down the hills and valleys, continually looking left and right. We came across a small stream at midday and were there quite a while. The sheep were very thirsty from their previous ordeal; their thirst hadn't been quenched by the morning dew while grazing. We did see indications that our stragglers had been through this area and were thankful that no other threatening foot prints could be seen. After proper rest, we continued on in a northerly direction.

A few sheep returned this day, usually at the most unexpected places. The path would open wider and appear easier going; something would cause us to cast a glance aside and we would see one of our sheep in the distance. We would collect our flock and herd them toward this runaway. Why

they took the narrower path in the first place I couldn't deci-
pher, but we herded the entire flock towards this new- found
member with the supposition that others had followed this
route also.

This routine occurred many times this day. I began to
develop the impression that it wasn't I that was leading the
sheep but that I myself was the one being guided. But sometimes your mind can invent things when left alone in the
hills.

We journeyed on. As the sun got lower in the sky, I began to look for an area for the sheep to lie down that night. I
found a suitable area near a rocky ridge, so Daniel and I prepared the location. We gathered fallen branches of various
sizes and arranged them to form a semblance of a pen. But
the sheep were very content now even though it was an unfamiliar setting, as if they had been here before. They were as
relaxed as if they were at home.

The sun continued its normal path and darkness came
upon us. We completed our tasks and arranged our cloaks
for bedding. Before long Daniel was comfortably asleep. The
extended travel this day had taken its toll on him. I arranged
his mantle around him to keep him warm throughout the
night. Even though we had a small fire going, it would still
get quite cool, especially higher up in the hills.

I remained awake, keeping watch while reconstructing
the previous days' events in my mind. How a man's plans can
suddenly change and he finds himself in such a different
situation.

I was leaning against a rock, turning over in my mind
this change in my plans for this grazing drive, and at the
same time gazing up at the stars on this cloudless night. Even
though the lights in the heavens were providing considerable
illumination, I began to notice that an extra light was being

cast into our area. It was coming from beyond the rocky ridge above us. I collected my shepherd's rod, took a cursory look at the flock, and started up the rocks to find the source of the light. Was there another shepherd in the area? Was I seeing the light from a fire at his camp? It was a strong light; maybe it was a larger group or some Roman soldiers. My mind quickly jumped to conclusions. I climbed up the rocks as silently as possible, for I also didn't want to rouse the sheep. The night was cool and the dew on the rocks made for a slippery condition against my sandals. I didn't want another mishap.

I climbed the rocks until I found a path which wound next to the rocks that rose above me. I continued on up the path. The light was getting brighter and radiating higher still above the rocks towards the heavens. I was almost to the top of the ridge where I would have an unobstructed view. Cautiously I crept forward. The path turned through an opening in the rocks, revealing the most unimaginable sight. A short distance away was a stairway, not just an ordinary stairway, but a large Golden Stairway—brilliant and lighting up the hillside, leading up to the heavens—the top of which I couldn't see. Angels of God were going up and down the stairway. At the bottom was someone wearing a robe brighter than anything on earth, sitting on a clear platform in a golden chair, a chair like a throne. I covered my eyes in case I should be struck dead for looking at this Godly image. But since I continued to exist, I took another look, as I was unable to control my wonderment. The angels descending the stairway were attending the seated figure and then would ascend back up to the heavens.

I watched for a time, and then my face became warm from the glow emanating from the Golden Stairway, so I took a few steps backward. As I retreated, my foot slipped and caught on a rock, causing it to roll away and uncover a hole. I couldn't see in the dark shadows because my eyes had adjusted to the brilliant light, and in an instant, my leg plunged into the hole. From what I can remember, it caused me great pain. In my agony, and fearful that I was falling off the cliff, I cried out, "God, have mercy on me!" I don't know all the events after this because as I fell, I must have hit my head on a rock, causing me to fall asleep for a while.

How long this unconscious state was upon me I am not sure, but I was awakened by powerful hands underneath my arms and body that effortlessly lifted me up. My head was still cloudy and my eyes were unable to focus, yet I remember being set down gently, so that I reclined against a rock. My legs and head were still sore.

As my vision returned, I became aware that a person was in front of me. His robe was bright; bright as a glowing light. Our eyes met and his seemed to penetrate my soul, but I wasn't afraid. He smiled at me, and then I realized that he was the one that the angels were attending at the bottom of the stairway. He said something quietly that sounded like a prayer which I couldn't comprehend, and then he put his hands over me. With one hand he touched my head, and with the other hand my leg, and said "Shemaiah, your sins are forgiven."[2]

Immediately, the pain in my head and leg were gone. I thanked him and then looked up to see who had lifted me up, but there was no one there. I then looked forward, but he was gone too. I looked around without getting up, but I was all alone. By now I was exhausted. I leaned back and quickly fell asleep.

Day 2 – Pierced

I was awoken by the morning sun. Since I was up on the ridge, I met the sun first. I peered over the edge and could see that Daniel was still sleeping. The sheep hadn't begun to stir, for they were still in the shadows. I checked my head and legs for injuries but found none. The previous night's events were still constantly in my thoughts, but they were so hard to comprehend that I wondered if they were just a dream.

I was up on the ridge, so I knew that much was true. I looked around and found the hole I had fallen into. Looking in, I could see that below the surface was an area large enough to hold several people. I hesitantly looked to see if the stairway was there. I don't know if my eyes were deceiving me, but I could faintly make out the same images I had seen in the dark. The sunlight allowed the stairway to be only slightly visible; in fact, the stairway was transparent. The throne at the bottom of the stairway was also visible, also transparent, and it was empty. However, the angels were still standing in place on the stairway ready to serve. Below the stairway, underneath the throne, was a platform as clear as crystal; the valley below could be seen through it.

I was very confused by this series of events, so I picked up my shepherd's rod, went back down the ridge and returned to Daniel and the sheep just as they were beginning to awaken. I didn't tell my story to Daniel since I didn't think he would understand and I didn't want to frighten him.

I placed my thoughts about the previous night in the back of my mind and went about the morning tasks. To our good fortune we realized we had stumbled onto a favorable range site, as the valley between the ridges contained a superior pasture. In fact, this morning we found a pair of our ewes grazing here. Since the herd was so content, I decided we would remain at this location, possibly for several days. Daniel appreciated a day at an easier pace as well.

When my other distractions had been eliminated, my thoughts again returned to the one who healed me. He had healed me with the touch of his hands and his words. However, they weren't 'magic words,' but "your sins are forgiven." How was this possible?

Was this an angel? But I had seen what appeared to be angels on the stairway and they were attending this man.

Was he a prophet? I remembered that a few years back, I had seen a rough-looking man near the Jordan River (John was his name) who told people they were full of sin, and that they must repent for the evil things they did and thought.

"Repent of your sins. Turn back to God!" he said.[3] If they believed him, and repented, he would take the people into the river and then bless them. Then he said that someone more important than he was coming: "The Kingdom of Heaven is near." He said that his job was to announce and prepare people for the coming of the Lord,[4] who would take away our sins. How could he take them away?

There were many stories lately about a man of God who was healing people. He had been traveling about the area for at least three years telling people about God (whom he called his Father), talking about Heaven and also healing people. Great crowds were drawn to him. Those who had heard him (especially the many that were healed) were convinced he was the promised Savior. Indeed, just before I left on this trip, my neighbor told me an incredible story about his friend

Timaeus in Jericho[5], and how his blind son could now see because of this man.

Was this the same person that the Jewish leaders in Jerusalem were trying to kill? That is what was being said among the people in the streets at the market in Jerusalem; that the Pharisees, chief priests and scribes (the lawyers) wanted to kill him. In fact, there was gossip that a reward would be paid for his capture.

Again I recalled what the man said last night: "Your sins are forgiven." How *was* this possible? Only God forgives sins. Was this God? But I saw him. If I had seen God, would I still be alive? As Moses had warned, God commanded that anyone who looks on him will surely die. But I was still alive and very thankful. Thankful that my leg was healed (I gave it a slap—better than ever!) Thankful that my head didn't have a bump—not even a bruise. So happy was I that I shouted, "Praise the Lord!" No sooner had the words left my mouth than I turned and there he was.

"Peace be with you!"[6] He said. Even though the sun was shining brightly, his clothes were brighter still. Immediately I fell to his feet, like a dead man. He then placed his hand on me and said, "Do not be afraid."[7]

I was only able to talk in a stammer, and with my eyes closed I said, "Thank you for rescuing me and healing me last night." I then opened my eyes and to my horror I saw his feet. There were holes in both of his feet! Not little holes but large holes, such as what would be made by a stake or a spike and then torn....how could he stand on those feet? Then I saw the hand that had been on my shoulder. It had a horrendous hole too, as did his other hand. Tears began to roll down my face and great sadness overwhelmed me, for I knew what these holes meant. These were the holes from a crucifixion; that is what the Romans do. This man had been crucified!

He saw my tears, and told me I was correct. "I was dead, but now I am alive forever!"[8] he said.

After I regained my composure and observed his hands and feet again, I brought forth a small amount of courage and asked this radiant figure, "Who are you? Why were you crucified?"

He explained that that was his purpose for coming. He was "the Son of Man, he came to serve and to give his life as a ransom to set men free."[9]

"I don't understand," I said.

He said that he came to save people, people of the entire world, from sin and death.

"How can I be saved?" I asked.

He told me to just believe in him. Believe that he came from God. Believe that he had been dead, but was now alive. Believe that he had risen from the dead.

"I can believe that," I said. "I can see that you have suffered and have been crucified. I've been to Jerusalem when they crucify people; the scene has always repulsed me. Nobody deserves to die that way. Only someone from God could survive."

Then I asked, "How did you survive the cross? Did you climb down? The Romans make sure that nobody leaves the cross alive."

"The crowds wanted me to come down from the cross," he said, "to confirm I was God's son,[10] but that was not my Father's will. The Romans did make sure I was dead. This wound in my side from the Roman spear is proof of that." Then he pulled open his robe and showed me; seeing the result of him having to endure being pierced caused me to be sick.

He then told me that after he had given up his spirit on the cross, he was taken down and placed in a tomb. Long burial cloths had been wrapped above and below him and a cloth put over his face. He was most certainly dead. The tomb was then sealed, closed by rolling a heavy rock across the opening. A guard unit was even positioned outside it to ensure that nobody disturbed the grave and his body. He lay there several days.

"When did all this happen?"

He replied, "It was just before Passover, on the 14th of Nisan."

I then recounted the strange storm with the pitch black sky and the heavens in turmoil.

"That was when the debt was being paid; the payment in blood that God required for the sins of the world. I stayed on the cross until all sins were paid for, until my mission was completed, until I could announce that it was finished."[11]

"Then the earth quaked."

And he nodded.

It was hard to comprehend everything. But he was here, so I could not help but believe.

I continued with my questions.

"How long were you in the grave?"

"A few days, so scripture could be fulfilled," he said. "I explained this to some friends yesterday, when traveling to Emmaus, reminding them of Hosea's words: 'After two days he will revive us; on the third day he will restore us, that we may live in his presence.'[12] For you see I lay down my life, only to take it up again.[13] I have authority to lay it down and authority to take it up again."[14]

I stared, mesmerized. This wasn't a braggart. This was someone who had true power: God.

"At the proper time, heavenly angels rolled the grave stone away. Early in the morning, the time that roosters crow. Yesterday."

"The beautiful day!" Then I recalled the rumbling which woke me.

He smiled and nodded again, and then he turned towards Daniel and smiled. All this time Daniel had been sitting near the sheep, kicking some rocks back and forth with his feet, but always with an ear towards the conversation. Normally he is very timid and uncomfortable with strangers, but this time he was uncharacteristically calm and smiled back.

Then Daniel said, "You are the Christ, the Son of the living God. You are Jesus."

"And you are blessed," Jesus said. "Nobody told you this; my Father in Heaven made this known to you."[15]

I was stunned. Daniel's speech is usually difficult to understand, but this was crystal clear. "You are the one John preached about. The Lamb of God, you take away the world's sins!"[16]

"Yes,' he said. "I am He."

But then he said that his time here was almost over, and that he would be returning to the Father soon. The angels were assisting him for a short while and then he would return home.

"I saw the Golden Stairway," I blurted out.

Then he informed me of where we were. I had lost track of reference points and become unsure of where I was when the earth quaked and the sheep deserted me.

"This area was well traveled, many years ago, by Abraham and Jacob. In fact, we are at the place where Jacob had his dream, the dream where he saw the same stairway and the angels ascending to Heaven and descending. It wasn't just something he imagined: it was real. We are east of where Bethel was and west of the ancient city of Ai, as Moses recorded."

I asked Jesus many questions that day, and I became weary from the revelations I was blessed with. Jesus, who is aware of everything, also noticed this exhaustion and said that was enough for today.

"We'll have more days for discussion," he said, "for I have *had* plans for you."

The day had passed quickly; the sun was getting lower in the sky. I turned to ask Daniel if he was hungry. When I turned around, Jesus was gone. In his place was a small fire with some fish cooking over it and some bread (the bread was made without yeast, for it was the Festival of Unleavened Bread).[17] I didn't take time to contemplate where the fish came from even though we weren't near a stream or lake. Daniel and I ate the fish and were very satisfied.

I herded the sheep together for the night. Later, Daniel fell asleep with the most pleasant look on his face: one of total joy. Earlier, Jesus had used the phrase "your joy will be complete."[18] Daniel had that joy.

When all was quiet, I again climbed up the ridge, this time with more caution. I could see the familiar glow cast across the rocks, but I still marveled when I saw the Golden Stairway. Angels were going up and down, and there, seated on the platform, was the same figure as before, the one who had been with us today: Jesus.

Day 3 – Plans

The singing of the many birds in the hills woke me
this day, and my thoughts immediately turned to the
conversation with Jesus, or as Daniel said, "the Christ, the
Son of God."

How could I be so fortunate to have the Son of God answering my questions personally, face to face? How could
anyone who has met Jesus not believe? Some have believed,
but many have not. How could they kill him? Sadness began
to sweep over me as I remembered the holes in his feet, and
his hands, and his side where the soldier's sword had pierced
him. But for all that suffering, he was alive. Yes, he had been
dead. But he was very much alive now. He *had* conquered
death. Could I also? I'll have to ask him about this.

Then I remembered the words he said just before He left.
He said, "I have plans for you." No, he said more than that.
He said, "I have *had* plans for you." What did he mean by
that? I hadn't planned on being here. This wasn't our normal
grazing tour. I've never brought sheep here before. The only
reason I ended up here is that the earthquake startled the
sheep and they ran.

But they didn't take the easiest paths. I had to redirect
my course many times as members of the flock were found
elsewhere. I slowly came to realize that the sheep were found
in a succession that guided me to this spot.

So when He said "I have *had* plans for you," what did he
mean? Was this journey *not* an accident—not a series of ac-
cidental events? Was I then destined to be here? But I had
choices the entire time. What a mystery this is—but I'm not

sure I'm ready for the answer to this. What I do know is that I'm here and Jesus knew it and planned for me to be here, and he said he has plans for me. Isn't that what Jeremiah said? "For I know the plans I have for you," declares the LORD, "plans to prosper you and not to harm you, plans to give you hope and a future."[19] I am sure they are plans for good, not for evil, but I am anxious—though I shouldn't be—just the same.

Daniel and I tended to the sheep. We took them out in to the fields; we wouldn't think of leaving the hills while Jesus was here, for he said he was returning to His Father soon. What a privilege to be here! How could anyone want to leave? But I did wonder about Meira and hoped she was getting better. I prayed to God for her healing: "Just as the blind man of Jericho received his sight, so let Meira be healed." After what I had already seen, I truly believed she would be healed.

I was watching the flock when suddenly I heard, "Peace be with you." When I saw Him, I instinctively fell to the ground. He had me rise and follow him, and I saw that he was carrying something that looked like long bags made of linen. He led me underneath a shade tree and set them down on a flat rock. He had two bags and he opened the ends of each. They contained scrolls. Were these the ancient texts that he referred to when he talked about the Scriptures that must be fulfilled? He unrolled one but it was blank, and he said the other was the same. Then I noticed a small jar next to the rock, and some quill pens lying next to it, but he hadn't been carrying these.

Not every shepherd can write, but my father insisted I learn, and Jesus knew this without asking. He then set about instructing me of the plans that he *had* for me; I was to write on the scrolls. That was all he said and then he left.

Now when the Son of God tells you to write, you write. But what was I to write? I stared at the blank scrolls in front of me, each a fine sheepskin scroll. I lifted the jar and saw that it was filled with writing fluid. The quills looked liked they were from eagles' feathers, and their tips were already cut and prepared for writing. I was accustomed to using reeds, but this would be far better. I looked at the rock and brushed my hand across it; it was very smooth. Everything was right in front of me: all that I would need.

I was so confused about what I should do, and fretted that I would disappoint Him. He had planned for me to be here, but what was I supposed to do? "Write." I was to write on the scrolls, but what?

For a while, I stared at the rock in front of me, then the hills around me, then the sky above me. I even got up and walked around the rock several times.

How did the old scripture writers, the prophets, get their inspiration to write? Often what they wrote didn't make sense until many years later, even centuries later, and still much is yet to be explained. Isaiah said many things that are hard to understand. Like that verse with the phrase that always caught my ear: "He was led like a lamb to the slaughter."[20] Then I realized that this had just come true—the crucifixion of Jesus! Oh, it was so clear now. But Isaiah wrote that more than 700 years ago. How did he know? How was he able to write that? Did he realize what he was writing or was he given a special vision?

Some writers retold their dreams. Jacob dreamed about the ladder to Heaven. Joseph had many dreams: about the sun and the moon and the stars bowing down to him, and about fat and skinny cows. Solomon had a dream and gained the gift of great wisdom (which he had asked for), and then received even more gifts for which he hadn't asked. I need to have some wisdom too. Jesus didn't say "Fall asleep, dream, and then write." He just said to write.

So I sat down again at the rock, picked up the quill, placed it cautiously in the jar of writing fluid, and then gently wrote on the scroll, "This record of events is from Shemaiah, a shepherd ..." and I continued on from there. I recounted the events Daniel and I experienced. I found choosing the proper words and writing to be a slow process, but I was persistent.

I didn't see Jesus anymore that day. But before going to sleep for the night, when it was dark and quiet, I did climb the ridge again and was happy and comforted to see him at the bottom of the stairway.

Day 4 – Trust

Choosing words to write is not only difficult for the mind, it's also time-consuming. It also means depending on Daniel to look after the sheep. However, I've never seen the sheep so contented, so Daniel's day was more relaxed. Jesus didn't make an appearance today, so I continued my work on the scrolls, hoping I was writing what I was supposed to be writing.

It seemed that when I didn't try so hard to find the words, what Jesus said came through most easily. So I stopped trying to control the process and let his will take over. I guess this was a step towards following Solomon's proverb, which says, "Trust in the LORD with all your heart and lean not on your own understanding."[21] For most people, myself included, that takes time to learn, but once you do, it will then be possible to "in all your ways acknowledge him, and he will make your paths straight."[22]

Now that I was instructed to write, we had no inclination to leave this location. In fact, it was just one of several reasons to remain here. In addition to the sheep being very content, our flock was increasing. With no effort of our own, our runaway sheep were returning. First two returned, then later, three more appeared. This was unnatural for sheep to do, especially since they had been scattered over quite a distance. Their return caused me to consider the possibility that they were being directed by heavenly shepherds.

Day 5 – T h e   W o r d

I was awakened this morning by the feeling that something was in our camp area. A shepherd must always be on guard to protect his sheep from harm, no matter what time of day or night. Wild animals can take horrific tolls on a flock, and with very little noise. Had this pleasant area allowed me to relax and forget my responsibilities? I jumped to my feet and grabbed hold of my shepherd's rod, but a quick examination found that we were in no danger at all. Our unknown guest was Jesus, sitting at the writing desk and reading the scroll.

"Well done," he said.

He smiled and said he liked what was there, and that I was doing good work. I apologized for not being much of a writer, confessing I also didn't know what to write.

He explained, "What you write comes from the Holy Spirit: His inspiration, God-breathed.[23] The prophets all wrote, such as Hosea and Joel and Jonah and *all* the others, but the words were *all* from God."

I also admitted to wondering if these scrolls would serve any purpose to anyone or if they were just for my benefit.

He laughed lightly and said, "Don't be concerned about that; you fill your mind with too many cares. Isaiah wrote about this when God pointed out to him how God's thoughts are not like man's thoughts and God's ways are beyond anything people could ever imagine. And as an example, just like rain and snow come down and nourish the plants and crops in the fields so they grow and feed his creation, so do the words go out and achieve His purpose. It never will go out and produce nothing—it always prospers.[24] Just as the Spirit is with the writer, it is also with the one who reads the words."

I then blurted out, "I try to choose the words carefully so they'll be productive."

Jesus paused, shook his head and then explained it another way to me. "Man's word is not like God's word; God's word has power. 'The Lord merely spoke, and the heavens were created. He breathed the word, and all the stars were born.'[25] God's word created everything; earth and every creature."

Then he astonished me by saying that *he* was the Word of God.[26] Once again I fell to his feet, unworthy to stand in his presence. Being a Jew, and having been instructed well, I knew that to say you are the Word of God is to say you are God. Maybe I was dense before, not realizing what he meant. Maybe it just needed to be hammered harder into my hardened heart. When Jesus said that he was the Word, I finally understood: He is God as he had said, so he and the Father are one. He was there at the beginning of creation because he is the creator. Nothing was created except by Him.

I now comprehended that when God's Spirit, who is God the Father and Jesus, inspired the writers of scripture with words, they were the author of the words and they, as one, were the authors of life.

My head was pounding with this revelation, and thoughts of unworthiness overwhelmed me. Jesus then, again, put his hand on my shoulder and understood my thoughts, without me outwardly expressing them, and said that I was worthy. That is why he, the word, became human and lived among us[27] and died for us and took away our sins.

Then I remembered that on the first night on the ridge when he healed me, he had said, "Shemaiah, your sins are forgiven." He died and paid the price for our sins so that we would be able to stand in God's presence.

After a quite a long silence Jesus smiled and said, "You must speak my words to them, whether they listen or fail to listen."[28]Then once again he impressed on me, "The word of God is alive and powerful. It is sharper than the sharpest sword, cutting between soul and spirit, being able to expose a person's innermost thoughts and desires.[29] Some will hear the message but the devil will come and take it away, blocking it from their thoughts with doubts, preventing them from believing. Some will be full of enthusiasm, but it won't last and they'll go back to their old ways. Some will just become too busy with their lives to even remember the message, casting aside its importance. But don't fret, there will be those who hear, believe, hold onto it daily, and then tell others as well."[30]

"So you also must tell others," he continued. "Don't hide it or keep it to yourself.[31] What I say is true; God's word is the truth. So continue to put down on the scroll what the Spirit has impressed on your heart and pray that the reader may believe and be saved."

"Prophecies that have been written for thousands of years will all come true," he added. "Some have already come true; many are coming true now. Take note, no matter what happens: the word of God stands forever."[32]

After our discussion, Jesus talked with Daniel. Daniel showed him around the field where the sheep were grazing and led him to his favorite ewes. He then showed him different flowers growing nearby, especially the daisies, which were his favorite. I could see him cautioning Jesus about the bees, and Jesus nodding appropriately at Daniel's concern. Some rocks were thrown and others overturned to show him insects that were hiding beneath. Daniel is an affectionate person; he is also perceptive, and shows it with his actions. After more smiling and laughing they said their goodbyes, and Daniel gave Jesus a big hug.

As Jesus walked by, he told me that I had plenty to think about for today, and though I would not see him until tomorrow, he would still be with me. That he would be close by was very comforting; the Psalmists often wrote about that.[33] But something else the psalmists said had new meaning: "I have put my hope in your word."[34]

Daniel and I prepared a meal, after which I went back to my task at the writing rock. The words came easier now.

The prophets of old had to expend so much energy in warnings of coming wrath. I was fortunate that I was able to write about what they could only hope for.

Day 6 – Foretold

Another glorious morning; I woke up overflowing with questions for Jesus. Daniel and I did our morning routines and then I continued with my recording of events on the scrolls. As I was writing, I kept looking around for Jesus to appear. I started to wonder if I would see him at all today, for the sun was high above my head now. But as I finished my final thought and set the quill down, he arrived—at just the right time.

He greeted us with his accustomed "Peace be with you." I had just started to ask my many questions when he held up his hand to stop me. He sat down on a rock and told me that he had been down into the towns appearing to certain people, proving that he is alive, raised from the dead, and that death's hold is broken.

"How many people have you shown yourself to?" I asked.

He said nearly a hundred since he left the grave, and there would be more before returning to his Father. Many were doubtful at first, but once they saw his hands and feet and the scar in his side they were convinced. Sometimes there were other signs that convinced them. He then told about a walk he made west of Jerusalem, to a small town called Emmaus, with Cleopas and his friend. It wasn't until they noticed how he blessed and broke the bread that they realized with whom they had been speaking.[35]

"Why didn't you tell them sooner?" I asked.

Jesus explained, "It was more important that they listen to what I said. If they'd known it was me, they wouldn't have listened as well. Their minds would have been clouded over with other thoughts. They were very upset about the crucifixion and confused about the events that had just happened in Jerusalem."

"What was it that you told them?"

"That all the events, including the suffering that the Christ had to endure, were necessary and had been foretold. I explained how sin had separated man from God, but because God truly loves his creation, he provided for salvation through his Son, and *only* through his Son. My coming as a man and suffering and then the victory over death were all part of God's plan from the beginning.

Then Jesus proceeded to tell me some of the stories. Many that he told were very familiar, and as he would begin I would wonder if I should record such well-known accounts when I wrote on the scrolls. However, as he told the story he pointed out details which I recognized but had never completely understood, and he would simply explain how they described him. Each story connected to the next, but they were not just any stories. These were from the Holy Scriptures. They covered thousands of years, from before the time of Abraham 2,000 years ago, and during the time of Moses 1,400 years ago, and David 1,000 years ago: different prophets telling different parts of the same story.

He began at the very beginning, when sin first separated man from God. This occurred when Adam and Eve disobeyed God's instructions (due to temptations from the serpent). That is when the battle with Satan began, and God responded. Among the punishments God declared, man would receive death and Satan would receive even worse. But here are the overlooked details: God also promised a redeemer through the offspring of Eve—his son Jesus (although it would be many generations later). God also stated that this redeemer would suffer.[36]

He told how as the people on earth increased in number, sin also increased. Many years after the flood, God announced his salvation plans again, promising his servant Abraham that everyone would "be blessed" through him[37] - and the path to the savior was through Abraham's son. The eventual salvation would be an unbreakable agreement between God and man.[38] Of course God was referring to His Son.

Just then Daniel started blowing his flute, which caused Jesus to pause. Daniel's flute was two reeds tied together with some holes carved into them. He would move his fingers back and forth over the holes, blowing as loudly as he could. He played much better now than he used to, but even so, it always got the sheep's attention—and anyone else nearby. Jesus smiled and laughed at the enjoyment Daniel got out of making plenty of noise, and the sheep's reaction as well.

"Now, Shemaiah, Jesus said. "I know you love your son. Well, Abraham had a son he loved too. But God had a test for him."

"A test? God was going to test him?"

"Yes. Isaac was a special son. Remember, I said the path to the savior was through Abraham's son."

"What subject was He going to test him on?

"God tested Abraham's faith: to show who was first in his life, he was to sacrifice Isaac. But God was demonstrating more than that."

What Jesus explained to me next makes the following scripture mean so much more: I felt like hitting myself in the head for not recognizing it sooner. The Scriptures record that Isaac questioned the sacrifice, and Abraham responded that "God will provide a lamb for the offering."[39] Now God *did* provide a lamb in place of Isaac, but he was really referring to the future, when His Son would take our place as an offering for our sins.

"I am glad that Abraham passed the test successfully. But I'm not sure I could have done as well," I confessed.

Jesus consoled me by saying, "God knows what you are capable of, don't fear."[40]

Then Jesus continued, reminding me of another time God demonstrated how all people would receive salvation, this also with a lamb. When God rescued the Israelites from their captivity in Egypt, the blood of a perfect and unblemished lamb was to be brushed on the doorposts of the Israelites' homes. This was the only way to prevent the Lord from striking down their firstborn: the angel of the Lord who would carry out this task would pass-over their home. [41]

This is such a well-known story, one we remember every year: how could we not realize its significance? It is clear now, Jesus would be our sacrificial lamb, our Passover lamb, and his blood would save us from death. The Savior's blood, shed on the cross, would save all mankind; death would not have a hold on those who believe in him. Now I know that Jesus is that lamb, and I realize that scripture has been fulfilled.

There are many references in scripture that mention the role of the lamb, and many others that don't refer to sacrifices but still point to a savior. Before Moses died, God gave him many instructions which he then gave to the Israelites, including the promise that he would raise up a prophet.[42] Jesus was to be this prophet.

Jesus pointed out so many references to me. One that makes everything so clear is what God told Nathan to tell David. He said, "When you die and are buried with your ancestors, I will raise up one of your descendants, your own offspring, and I will make his kingdom strong"[43] and "I will secure his royal throne forever. I will be his father, and he will be my son."[44] David's own writings are filled with numerous references to Jesus. [45]

Then Jesus mentioned that there are other places in scripture that talk about how he would be born, where he would be born, where he would live, and other aspects of his life. That left me dumbfounded; I asked him for examples.

Jesus then said about his birth, "Isaiah described my life quite thoroughly. He was greatly used by the Spirit, especially when he talked of my birth. Surely you read that 'the Lord himself will give you a sign: The virgin will be with child and will give birth to a son, and will call him Immanuel.'[46]

I had heard those words, but never understood them.

"Isaiah also said these wonderful words: 'For to us a child is born, to us a son is given' and 'he will be called Wonderful Counselor, Mighty God, Everlasting Father, Prince of Peace.'"[47]

Jesus pointed out that the prophet Micah told where he would be born: in Bethlehem.[48] Then he referred again to Isaiah, saying he wrote that he would live in Nazareth and Capernaum.[49]

Jesus continued this detailed interpretation of the Scriptures for quite a while. As he continued on, my amazement grew. I had heard all the old Scriptures he quoted before, but when it was all put together, it read as one story. It was marvelous. All of it was quoted with authority and no hesitation. My questions were answered by one who knew the answers, as if he had written the verses himself—which he had.

I went to my writing rock to record as much information as I could. I lifted the lid to the small jar with the ink to begin writing. (Even though I've been doing a considerable amount of writing, the ink never recedes.) While the stories are very familiar, their meaning has never been clear until now. I am highly honored to have the privilege of recording this knowledge, but at the same time I seem lacking for the task. How can I retell so much of the scripture which foretells God's plan for the world through his Son? There was so much that he told me. He knew I couldn't remember it all, only a small portion actually, but Jesus made me realize that it wasn't important to know all the details. It was more important to believe that it was true: that he is God's son.

Having Jesus point out different times in scripture covering more than 2,000 years makes you consider your own place in time. It's easy to think that what occurs now is what matters, that the past is not as important as what happens now. But that is not correct. God exists now, but He existed long ago too—He always existed. We are like a wildflower in the field;[50] here today and tomorrow we're gone. To think that God, a God of order, lets everything run with no plan is an ill-conceived notion. God has plans and his hand is on everything; preparations for his Son's arrival were quite involved.

So what does this mean? If we are only here for a moment in time, and if God's plans span thousands of years, and we're part of that purpose of those plans, then God *does* love us. He has compassion on us, his servants,[51] and He cares about His creation. I am part of His creation; we are all part of His creation.

Day 8 – Sharing

Yesterday I observed the Sabbath, rested and gave thanks to God.

Today, Jesus said he would be spending time with his disciples, the eleven. (There had been twelve.) There was one in particular that he needed to see yet, one who was absent when Jesus presented his risen self on the day he left the grave. Thomas is his name. He's quite boisterous about his doubts, too. But he will be convinced: the scars in Jesus' hands and feet are very convincing. Even so, as Jesus says, "There will be many who will not see me or the scars and will believe; they will be blessed."[52]

Tonight, we found fish prepared and cooking over a fire again. There was also bread, this time baked with yeast, for the Feast of Unleavened Bread was now over. Whenever Jesus visits the disciples, he always brings back fish. But this time there was much more fish and bread than just the two of us could eat. Why was there so much? Was Jesus going to eat with us?

Then I noticed someone walking out in the field, the same field where the sheep were grazing. I started to reach for my shepherd's rod, but the sheep weren't acting nervous, and a thief doesn't usually bring food for his victims.

The stranger seemed to sense my stare and turned towards me, smiled and waved. We approached each other and he introduced himself as Nathanael, adding that many call him Bartholomew. He said he was one of Jesus' twelve. Jesus had brought him here, then left, telling him that his friend would take care of him. He commented that I must have been aware of his appointment for he could smell the meal that had been prepared.

"That wasn't our doing," I said. "The Lord provided. He's teaching me not to worry about what we will eat."[53]

Nathanael nodded; he must have recognized the lesson.

We sat down and enjoyed our specially prepared meal. While we watched the colorful display of the setting sun, I asked Nathanael how he had come to be with Jesus.

"My good friend Philip brought me to Jesus," he said. "It is fascinating how it happened. I am from Cana of Galilee, the son of Tolmai. My father has always impressed upon me the importance of studying scripture, which I did, and I looked forward to the arrival of the Messiah. One day Philip said to me, 'We have found the one Moses wrote about in the Law, and about whom the prophets also wrote—Jesus of Nazareth, the son of Joseph.'[54] I immediately went with him. I admit that I was doubtful because I didn't think anything good could come from Nazareth. When I met Jesus, he said some kind things to me, and then surprised me by saying that he had seen me under the fig tree before Philip called me. Now we had just traveled quite a distance to see Jesus, we hadn't seen anyone in front or behind us as we walked, and he was here when we arrived. My hope was a doubt no longer as I realized immediately, and I even confessed it aloud, saying: 'Rabbi, you are the Son of God; you are the King of Israel.'"[55]

"What did he say," I asked.

"Well, he laughed and questioned that I believe because of this? Then he said that I would see greater things than this, which I have over and over again: the many healing miracles, feeding thousands, and then defeating death—

coming out of the tomb and living again. He told you that we can all live with him in eternity also, didn't he?"

I nodded and said that he did.

"When Jesus first said I would see greater things than this," Nathanael continued, "he also said something that I always will recall: 'I tell you the truth, you shall see Heaven open, and the angels of God ascending and descending on the Son of Man.'"[56]

Now I knew why Jesus had brought Nathanael here. I looked at Daniel and he smiled back; he knew what Jesus had done also. Jesus fulfills all his promises and this, too, he would fulfill. Even though angels were serving him now on the stairway, I was certain this scene would be repeated in Heaven as well.

We finished our meal and Nathanael told us stories of his time with Jesus. He confirmed events that I thought were just people's wild imaginations, and shared many more amazing stories that I hadn't heard before. I asked many questions, even a few about his final days, but it was so upsetting to all of us (especially Nathanael, for the details were too vivid in his mind) that I insisted that he stop.

But extraordinary events are not easy to keep within oneself, and as the sun disappeared and darkness settled in, Nathanael began to tell us about what happened on those days surrounding the crucifixion.

"Jesus had told us many times that on the third day he would be raised from the dead,[57] but we were so thick-skulled that we couldn't comprehend what he was saying. He spoke in parables so much that we had trouble understanding all that he said. But it turned out that he was talking plainly and we let it pass through us. He said it many times, too. He tried to say it even simpler to us; he said, 'In a little while you won't see me anymore. But a little while after that, you will see me again.'[58] He couldn't have said it more simply."

I tried to console Nathanael by saying that nothing like this had ever happened before, but then he replied, "We should have known. He had great power, even over the dead. I can recall at least three times right now. First, Jesus commanded his friend Lazarus out of a tomb, and he had been dead a couple of days.[59] He also healed Jairus' daughter; they said she had died too.[60] Then there was that woman's son—in Nain—we had met her on the road.[61] They were on the way to bury him. Jesus touched the coffin and all of a sudden the man sat up and started talking—that gets your attention. But after seeing him heal so many people, maybe we just thought...I guess we didn't think."

Nathanael sighed deeply, and then continued.

"Well, those last days, after we arrived at Jerusalem with the crowds shouting and cheering and praising him when he rode in on a donkey...I don't know where he got the donkey. We never traveled with one. This all happened so fast."

"That night we had a nice meal—you know, celebrating the Passover—and we were still charged up from the crowd and a little full of ourselves. But Jesus was so serious, like he knew it was his last meal. After the meal, we went out across the Kidron valley to this olive garden, Gethsemane. Jesus liked to go there to pray. At one point he had us stop and he took Peter and also James and I believe John with him and went a little further into the garden."

"We waited a while and then all of sudden this group of Roman soldiers and ruffians with torches and clubs came up the path and passed us. Judas, one of the disciples, was with them. Before we could do anything, they had arrested Jesus and were headed back to the city. We proved our bravery by hiding in the bushes and running the first chance we got. We were so disappointing. Peter and John followed the crowd at a distance, but Peter, in spite of all his previous boasting, didn't prove to be very brave, either. Earlier, Jesus had mentioned what Peter would do. At the time, I couldn't imagine a situation where Peter would cower and then deny Jesus. I thought we were all a tough bunch, but there I was, running away to hide, and I wasn't alone."

Nathanael paused to rub his eyes before continuing.

"The rest all happened so fast. Before the day was over Jesus was spiked to the tree—it was awful. But seven days ago, some of the women with us went to the tomb where they had buried him and came back to tell us that it was empty. We were all locked up in a friend's home; we had nowhere else to go. These women even recounted seeing an angel there, who said: "He has risen from the dead and is going ahead of you into Galilee. There you will see him,"[62] but we didn't believe them. So Peter and John ran out the door to go see for themselves. The rest of us stayed behind, except for Thomas. I don't know where he went. Then one of us said that he too remembered Jesus saying, "But after I have risen, I will go ahead of you into Galilee."[63] Now we were very confused and we spent a considerable time discussing this."

"Peter and John came back shortly, telling us it was true what the women said: all that was left in the tomb were some strips of linen and a burial cloth for his head.[64] Peter then said he needed to think and he left the house. The rest of us stayed there. We discussed whether we should go to Galilee, but as the day wore on, we never left the house. We just stayed there in Jerusalem."

"That night—oh praise God, that night. Peter came back to the house. I should say he about knocked the house down when he crashed through the door. He was shouting and saying, "It's true! It's true! I have seen the Lord!"[65] And then Cleopas and his friend burst in saying the same thing. We locked the doors and tried to quiet everyone down; we didn't want to rouse the entire city."

"Then we heard someone say, 'Peace be with you.'[66] We turned to see Jesus standing there. At first we were afraid, thinking we were seeing a ghost, but he convinced us and we calmed down. He even ate some fish. Then he filled us with his spirit and told us to forgive sins,[67] and then he left. What a day!"

It was getting dark now and I could see lights glowing above the ridge, which I had become accustomed to seeing. I told Nathanael to follow me, that he needed to see something. We wrapped our cloaks around us, as the evening air was getting cooler, and the three of us carefully made our way up the rocks. I cautioned them regarding the hole that I had fallen into and told them about the first time I saw Jesus. We progressed down the path and approached the end of the rocks. As we made the final turn, the sudden glow caused Nathanael to stop. He looked back at us and we nodded our approval to continue. I tried to prepare Nathanael, telling him that he was about to see something unlike anything of this world.

When he stepped out from the rocks, he saw the Golden Stairway, the angels ascending and descending, and Jesus on the platform, sitting in his royal chair. Nathanael lowered himself to his knees—all three of us did—and tears began to roll down his face. He kept repeating, "I tell you the truth, you shall see Heaven open, and the angels of God ascending and descending on the Son of Man."

We watched for what seemed like hours, mesmerized by this heavenly sight. After we finally climbed down the rocky ridge, we readied the area for the night. Nathanael stayed with us, and in the morning I awoke to hear him climbing up the ridge for another glimpse of the magnificent stairway. After all he had witnessed during the past few years, one would think he was prepared to grasp what he was seeing, but his smile and the glazed-over look in his eyes showed that the glory of the Son of God was worthy of our praise and adoration. I would have to agree.

Day 9 – Fearless

We spent the morning having breakfast with Nathanael and listening as he shared with us more astounding stories of Jesus, intermixed with exclamations of joy since he was still overflowing with the wonder of seeing Jesus, the angels and the stairway.

Daniel and I enjoyed his companionship, but after a while Nathanael found it necessary to depart and return to Jerusalem. He didn't want to worry the other apostles, lest they fear he was arrested by the Romans.

"We will be heading up to Galilee as we were instructed by Jesus," Nathanael said. "Peter is longing to go fishing so we'll probably be in his boat on the Sea of Galilee soon.[68] I'll go with if he does. We all need to get out; we've been locked in our rooms for too long. We try to get out some though, usually just before dark, but we must use caution in getting back through the Jerusalem gates at night."

We said farewell and Nathanael went on his way.

Jesus appeared later and we related our experiences with Nathanael. I mentioned showing him the stairway. He smiled and nodded his approval, but I know he already knew about it. He was pleased that everything went well.

We wondered if Nathanael would have trouble finding his way but Jesus assured us that the journey would be easy. Jesus said that he had traveled near this area when he was a boy with his mother and earthly father.

"Every year they would go to Jerusalem to the Feast of the Passover. The journey was long," he explained, "for the caravans avoided Samaria by traveling from Nazareth, around or sometimes across the Sea of Galilee, to Jericho and then to Jerusalem; the last stretch was near here."

"In fact," he added, "on one of those trips, when I was twelve, I caused my parents much consternation. When they started homeward, my parents thought I was with others, but actually I had remained in Jerusalem at the temple. They traveled for an entire day before they came to realize that I was absent. They returned to Jerusalem, and after a long search, they found me in the temple court asking and answering questions."

Jesus then hesitated and said his final journey was also near here. After healing the blind man in Jericho (which must have been the man Timaeus that my neighbor told me about), he passed nearby on his way to Jerusalem. But then he stopped and said that we would talk more about that some other time.

Jesus then brought the conversation back to Nathanael, referring to him as "a genuine son of Israel—a man of complete integrity."[69]

I asked, "Why are the disciples in Jerusalem and not with you?"

"My time here is almost over," he replied. "Soon I will leave this place and return to the Father, and they will have to go on without me. Right now they are weak and scared, but they will become strong and brave."

He then explained that before he died on the cross, he had instructed them: "After I have risen, I will go ahead of you into Galilee."[70] Again, when the women saw him at the tomb, they were afraid too. So he said to them plainly, "Do not be afraid. Go and tell my brothers to go to Galilee; there they will see me."[71] But even then they were scared and hid behind locked doors.

The disciples' lack of courage was now commonly known, for after Jesus had walked with Cleopas and his friend to Emmaus, and after their eyes were opened and they recognized who they were talking to, they too knew where to find the disciples; they returned to Jerusalem.[72] Jesus also went to Jerusalem to present his resurrected body to most of the disciples.

"But that is alright," Jesus said, "God knows what's in their hearts; He doesn't judge what others see.[73]. There is a purpose in everything. Their weakness will be replaced with God's strength and power. God's power works best in weakness.[74] So their weakness may be known now, but they will not remain weak."

Jesus stood and motioned for me to follow. I glanced at Daniel to check on what he was doing and could see him leading a few sheep to a small stream. Jesus assured me that Daniel's guardian would watch over him.

I followed Jesus a short distance down the path I had walked when I first arrived. The sun was low then and I was looking out for my sheep, so the surroundings were unfamiliar. Jesus turned and walked through some tall grass, stepped around some thistle and then ducked around some wild olive trees. He stopped, and when I caught up with him, I saw that the hills dropped off suddenly, leaving an unobstructed panoramic view.

He looked intently into the distance, pointing out Jerusalem, and then he continued discussing the disciples. It was if he could actually see them when he said: "Right now they think I am not with them. They feel alone. They won't be alone for long. I will send God's Holy Spirit to be with them, but the Spirit cannot come until I go."[75] (Once again he mentioned leaving. He was very clear about that. He would be returning to Heaven to be with his Father—God.) "When the

Holy Spirit comes to them they will become stronger. They are already becoming stronger because they have seen me die and have seen me come back from the grave."

"When the Holy Spirit comes, they will no longer hide their faith but will proclaim it everywhere. They will stand up in front of all people, and leaders, too: kings and governors. They will profess God's salvation though his Son, and many will believe because they had been cowardly before and now they are fearless and persistent in preaching their message. But they will also be hated by people everywhere because of me," Jesus explained. "They will be arrested and brought to trial."

He stunned me with what he said next: "They will be handed over to be persecuted and put to death.[76] Their new boldness will reinforce the truth, even to their deaths, because they cannot deny the truth. They will convince people with their deaths, because they know that no one dies to protect a lie. No man does that. They have seen the truth. They will stand true to the end because God will be with them through the Holy Spirit."

"When he, the Holy Spirit, comes," Jesus said, "he will convince the world of the meaning of sin, because they do not believe in me; of true goodness, for I am going away to the Father; and of judgment, for Satan who rules this world has been judged."[77]

I asked, "How will they know what to say?"

"The Holy Spirit; he will be their teacher and will bring to their minds all that I have said to them.[78] The spirit will speak plainly about me and therefore the disciples will also speak plainly about me, for they were with me during my entire ministry on earth."[79]

"When will they receive the Holy Spirit?" I asked.

"After I leave," he said. "They will go to Galilee for a while and I will see them there, then I will send the disciples back to Jerusalem to wait for the gift my Father promised.[80] Repentance and forgiveness of sins will be preached in my name to all nations, beginning at Jerusalem."[81]

I then asked, "Did you really mean 'even to their death?' You said: 'be persecuted and put to death.'"

"That is true," he said. "I told these men: 'No servant is greater than his master. If they persecuted me, they will persecute them also.'[82] I'll tell you now, some of them they will kill, even crucify, some will be flogged, even pursuing them from town to town to catch them.[83]"

"This will happen to the eleven?" I asked.

"The eleven will become twelve again to fulfill the Scriptures.[84] Persecution will occur to the chosen and to many others who believe; even to another of my mother's sons. But they will achieve great purposes before they die and with their deaths."

"How will they die?" I timidly asked. Then Jesus gave me insight that was hard to listen to:

"One will preach to the Scythians and Thracians and then be crucified in Achaia."

"One will preach far east of here, in India, before he is crucified." (I gasped when he said that I know him. This had to be Nathanael. Somewhere, down in the hills below us, in the direction we were now looking, he was walking back to Jerusalem. He was so happy this morning; thinking that he would eventually suffer so horribly brought tears to my eyes. When Daniel asks me what Jesus said today, I'll omit this; Daniel had quickly become found of Nathanael.)

Jesus continued: "One will be stoned to death nearby in Jerusalem."

"Herod will put one to death by the sword, also in Jerusalem."

"One will preach in many places and then be crucified in Hierapolis."

"Another will also preach in many places before being thrust through with a spear in a town also in India."

"One will be crucified in Rome."

"Have you told any of them how they will die?"

"I'll tell Peter soon; how he will be made to stretch out his hands like I did.[85] He is the only one I will tell, Shemaiah."

"What about the others who help the eleven?" I asked.

He paused for a moment, and then said: "Yes, they too will suffer. One will be stoned in Jerusalem.[86]

"One who will preach and write to many, especially to the Gentiles, he will die by the sword also, in Rome. He'll persecute my believers at first, and then he'll believe and follow me. He'll suffer much for my name."[87]

"And your brother?"

"Yes. At first he didn't believe, either,[88] but I have shown myself to him and now he believes.[89] He will also be stoned to death in Jerusalem."

"Will they *all* die by the hands of others?"

"No. There will be three, even four, who will not suffer by man to their death. But one will spend many days alone on an island before he returns to Ephesus to spend his last days before he enters into glory."

"Their fearlessness will show that their faith is genuine— it is the truth. Satan will carry out his work through many, using any method to convince people that I don't exist," Jesus said. "But many will believe."

He then explained that many throughout all the ages will be strong in faith and thus suffer rather than deny him.[90]

We stood in silence for a while, and I sensed that Jesus was in conversation with his Father. After a bit he smiled, turned and said it was time to go. We made our way back to the camp and found Daniel contentedly turning over rocks in the stream.

Now, sitting at my writing rock, I am anything but content. But resolutely, I carry out the task assigned to me. I solemnly record the fate of the disciples to this scroll. Cowards no longer, they will fearlessly preach the truth. My heart still doesn't always accept the fact that this life on earth is not permanent, that death comes to all, and for some—those filling Godly purposes, life can end so violently. Lord, give me the faith to be as strong as these.

Day 11 – Pride

My mind was still spinning, even though it had been two days since I had heard Jesus' description of the sacrifice the apostles will make, sacrificing their very lives by going out and speaking about Jesus. I was deep in thought, contemplating how a person could do that, could be so fearless…unless they were so sure that no harm could befall them, at least no everlasting harm.

I didn't hear Jesus approach. He startled me when he answered my thoughts, saying "Don't be afraid of those who want to kill your body; they cannot touch your soul. Fear only God, who can destroy both soul and body in hell."[91] He then explained that the Spirit will give the apostles strength and power so that they won't be afraid.

In fact, he said, "they will look forward to being with me in Heaven.[92] Their motivation for taking the message out into the world will be their love for others, just as God showed his love for his people by sending me to die for them, even though they were so sinful. [93] The apostles will demonstrate that they are my disciples by loving others."[94]

He continued: "The love they will show to others will be similar to what I did during my ministry. They will heal many people, even raise people from the dead.[95] They will tell people to repent, but mainly they will tell about the death and resurrection of God's Son, and what that means for them: peace with God and eternal life. When the disciples die, they will be going home to the Lord, a place I will prepare for them. As long as they are here they will be living as strangers. But when death approaches, they won't be afraid, they will see Heaven open. I'll be waiting for them, standing at God's right hand."[96]

A peace filled me as I absorbed what Jesus was saying. I looked out across the field at the sheep. The sheep were like me and very much at ease here. Stragglers were still appearing. The flock was gradually increasing, slowly getting back to the original number, but we still had many absentees. As the lost sheep reappeared, they settled in with their companions and were relaxed as well. They didn't really creating much more work for us, or I should say for Daniel, since I was working on the scrolls. Daniel still found plenty of time for climbing on the rocks and trees and uncovering insects. Then a thought entered my mind, causing me to start.

"Will the Kingdom of God be for all people, even people like Daniel?" I asked.

Jesus then assured me, "Yes, people like Daniel will be welcome. Furthermore," Jesus emphasized, "Daniel proclaimed his faith in me from the beginning—even before *you* did."

He pointed at me, then continued.

"The Spirit is already at work in him; that is how you were able to understand him so well that second day. When Daniel professed that I was the Christ, what he was speaking was understandable to you, but to him it was as if he was speaking another language: he was showing the power of God's spirit.[97]

"He may always be like a child in your eyes but he also has a faith like a child."

Jesus then stated to me what he had said many times to the disciples: "God's kingdom belongs to those who are like these children." He then emphasized with utmost compassion, "Anyone who doesn't receive the Kingdom of God like a child will never enter it."[98]

"How do *we* become like little children?" I asked.

"I will tell you not how to act like children but how to trust like a child." Then he said, "Children are a gift from God[99] and a blessing from God.[100] A little child trusts in his parents to be cared for and provided for completely, so much that he doesn't even know to think about it. As children grow in years, they begin to put themselves in charge, moving away from their parents; a child cannot always drink milk.[101] Much of this is natural and healthy and part of maturing. A child will grow up to be like his parents—an adult—but the adult will never grow to be like God."

"However, many grow to believe they know quite a bit, and pride sets in. Often it is the case that man believes he doesn't need God, that he can go forth by himself. Satan assists men in this wickedness of pride. In all his thoughts there is no room for God, over time thinking that there is no God or even that God is dead.[102] But be warned, the LORD has a day in store for all the proud and arrogant, for those who think they deserve to be highly honored (and they will be humbled)."[103]"Pride is a very old problem; an ancient battle, between Satan and God."

"A battle?" I questioned. "Where is this battle?"

"It is all around you—you can't see the battle, but you see its results. You should be aware that Satan is the spirit at work in the hearts of those who refuse to obey God.[104] Satan is the commander in this world, but he will be cast out."[105]

"When did it begin?"

"The battle began with Adam disobeying God's commands and it was costly to him.[106] Man continued to move his thoughts away from God and man's life got difficult. That is not the relationship that God intended.

"Man was made to be dependent on God. God was to be the most important priority in his life and He made it very plain, even putting it in writing."[107]

Jesus then related how he made this clear during the past three years, repeating often the two most important commandments of God, the first being "You must love the Lord your God with all your heart and with all your soul and with your entire mind."[108]

I had heard that saying many times from the Hebrew teachers and even more often from my mother. I thought that was common knowledge, simple as child's play to comprehend, so I boldly said: "Doesn't everyone know that God is most important?" I asked.

The answer I received was blunt, explaining what all people really are, and what I am: a sinful generation. Wherever man puts his time and effort, his trust and his devotion, becomes his god. Satan works to remove trust in the one true God[109] and replace it with something else: power,[110] possessions[111] or security.[112] Many try to acquire these using money: money for power, money for possessions, or money for security. For them, the acquisition and accumulation of money becomes their god. Money itself isn't evil, just the extreme desire for it.[113]

"None of these are what God desires for us to seek. We are to seek his kingdom and his righteousness.[114] You can't pursue money with all your efforts and pursue God with all your efforts," Jesus explained.[115]

"Yes, man is to work, but God will be the provider. It is God who created everything and controls everything,[116] and He knows what we need.[117] Don't you think he has the resources to provide for his people? All the silver and gold is his,[118] every animal of the forest is his, the cattle on a thousand hills[119] and everything else.

Jesus added, "The second commandment that is most important and what the entire law and all the demands of the prophets are based on is: 'Love your neighbor as yourself.'[120] "When you do prosper, and are generously blessed, and this is from God, then don't use this excess to become puffed up, but help your neighbor who is in need. Let your love of God be expressed: that is His intention. Don't turn your back on your neighbor; there may be a time when others will be instruments of God's love to bring aid to you."

"If you seek God's kingdom and faithfully obey the commands to love God and to serve him with all your heart and soul, you will receive what you need and be satisfied. But those who turn away to other gods to be satisfied will find God's anger.[121]

"That seems so simple," I said, "but there is so much turmoil in the world. Does that mean that people never put their trust in God?"

"People, even nations, have followed God's instructions and received His blessings. At first they are thankful and offer praises for what God has bestowed upon them. The nation or city and its people will follow God for a while. But then they will go their own way. God tries to prevent this. He has sent many people, often called prophets, to rebuke them and make them change their ways. Some have even repented when their sin was made apparent and their judgment announced. They turned back to God and he spared them."

"Whom did God spare? Who turned back?" I asked.

"One example is the great city of Nineveh—one hundred and twenty thousand people—even the king repented."[122] "They listened to Jonah, when he finally arrived there."

"But Nineveh... Nineveh no longer exists. It can't even be found," I said.

Then Jesus informed me that Nineveh, even though they repented, returned to their terrible ways again and received judgment.[123]

"He is a jealous and avenging God. He will take vengeance when filled with wrath.[124] Be warned, when God is angry, the earth trembles; the nations cannot endure his wrath."[125]

"This is the result of pride?" I asked.

"Yes. Nations will use their intelligence to become successful and wealthy, very wealthy. Then they'll trade with other countries to become even wealthier. Great wealth makes a person or a country and its leaders very proud. Their pride swells their minds and makes them think they are incredibly important, as if they are a god. God doesn't allow them to continue with such great self-importance for very long, and so he opens the door to their enemies and they bring down the magnificence that pride has created. The destruction is violent and fatal. Those who had so much pride before won't appear to be much of a god as they meet their demise.[126] There have been many cities and nations that achieved prominence, but without recognizing God their reign always comes to an end. The only kingdom that lasts, the only kingdom that is eternal, is God's kingdom."[127]

"Don't rulers always have plenty of pride?"

"Yes, but there have been exceptions; King David is one. His heart was in the right place.[128] You must realize that God did not intend for people to be ruled by kings. That was an outcry from the people: it was a rejection of God as their king, and in their folly, they chased after other gods as well.[129] But the people were warned; warned what having an earthly king would mean. He would make many demands. From among his own people, some would be taken to work for the king; some as servants, others to rule over their own people. Some would be forced to serve in his army while others would be commanded to produce food or weapons and equipment. He would even lay claim to their land as he desired, even if it was filled with their own crops or animals, or of those who worked for them. He would also require a tenth of their flocks. In essence, they would become the king's slaves.[130]

"God desired to protect and lead and provide, but Satan led people to choose a different way. God gave commands that if carefully followed, by both people and nations, would result in blessings from God. But Satan encourages people to want more. God knew that and gave them rules to protect them. If their fellow Israelite or brother required assistance, then they could lend him money—but at no interest—and these debts were to be cancelled every seven years. Lending to foreigners and charging interest *was* allowed, even beyond the seven-year period. And most importantly, God strictly forbade borrowing from other nations."[131]

"Why are there so many rules about lending?"

"The people with money will rule over those who don't have it. [132] This results in the poor becoming unable to prevent themselves from becoming like slaves. That happens with people and nations."

"God's people should show love: don't be hardhearted or tightfisted toward your poor brother. Since everything is from God, what you receive is a blessing from God, so open your hands and give freely.[133] Remember, you are also to give a portion back to God. You may think you don't have enough, but put God to the test! He will pour out blessings so great you won't have enough room to take it in. Try it![134]

"Now, regarding nations, do not borrow from other nations. Other nations don't know my Father; do not become their servants. God does not want you to be like the tail, and another the head; somebody else on top and you on the bottom.[135] Remember how I just said that God opens the door to your enemies?"

"But we don't follow any of those rules now," I said.

"…and the nations cannot endure his wrath," was Jesus' reply.

"Do you remember what Isaiah said?" Jesus then asked.

"He said so much." By now I was overwhelmed with the difference between what man does and what God desires.

"Isaiah said 'The government shall be on his shoulders.'"[136]

"That means you shall rule over the government?" I questioned. "The government pursued you to your death in Jerusalem."

Jesus nodded his head, and then said, "But the priests and the religious leaders did have a big part, too."

"So which government does Isaiah mean?"

"All of them. When I return I will reign over the entire world. Until then, the governments will work against me and against God. With Satan's assistance, they will try to make the true God small."

"How do you make God small?"

"By reducing the importance of God in people's lives, reducing to the point that God becomes nothing more than an occasional thought, or placed in a box and not allowed to interfere with everyday affairs, reasoning that things that you can see are more important than things that are not visible. Keeping belief in God to oneself becomes the rule, and Satan further distorts the belief that God has no place or that he is not even real. But they will allow foreign gods a place, even honor and worship them. The Scriptures are filled with examples of this. But those who believe the truth—they will persecute them and they will persecute those who follow me. There will be much tragedy."

"Just like with the disciples?" I said.

"Yes, but much more so.[137] They'll do more than just persecute, they'll also work to change their faith. Getting people to depend and put their faith in anything but God: faith in money or faith in a person or even faith in a government. Anything but faith in God or worship of God is the devil's goal."[138]

"Pride will make it very difficult for rulers of a government to put allegiance to God first, but that is what He commanded because that is what is best. Gideon realized it. Even though he might not have acted the way he talked, he at least got the words right when he said who really is in charge—not kings—"only the LORD will rule over you.""[139]

"So what should we do?" I asked.

"Turn away from your prideful ways, be humble like me. Pray and seek God. Stop doing what is wrong, what is evil. God knows what you're doing. He hears you, but He will forgive you if you ask. He can repair the nations too;[140] if they obey him, he'll set them above the others."[141]

"And if we follow God's commands?" I asked.

"You will receive blessings on top of blessings throughout the entire country, and receive prominence higher than all the nations on earth. There are so many blessings God has for those who believe,[142] but a person needs to change from this proud thinking and become humble. Those who humble themselves and believe will receive eternal life."[143]

Then Jesus stressed in a very personal way, "God considers you His children, if you receive him and believe in him.[144] Trust God like a little child trusts his parents. Humble yourself like a child and be more concerned about having a place in the kingdom of Heaven."[145] He repeated one more time: "Put your trust in God; trust also in me."[146]

Our conversation was interrupted by loud singing in the field in front of us. Daniel was swinging his staff and marching back and forth in song, with no apprehension at all. Jesus was enjoying Daniel's performance, mentioning how David showed his joy by shouting and dancing also.[147] Then, just when I thought he was finished talking about children, he firmly said there was more to discuss about children—but that we'd do that another time.

D a y   1 2   –   E n v y

I was moping around the field this morning. I had been berating myself for the responses that came out of my mouth yesterday when Jesus was telling me about God's displeasure with pride and what should be most important. I had said that it was simple and obvious that God should be the priority in a person's life. Yes, it was easy to say, but had I done it? Of course not. And that is why I was kicking myself today.

I, too, have envied those people with so much pride because they were so successful, regardless of their evil ways. No illness or injury ever slows them down; they're always full of energy. Problems that occur to others never happen to them.

They don't even try to conceal their proud manner; in fact, they flaunt it. But because of the way they treat others, they aren't very pleasant to be around. In fact, I have seen their pride expand to the point where they even taunt God.

Unfortunately, I wasn't the only one who wondered if God was aware of these people or if maybe it was acceptable to be this way. I had seen these wicked people having a good life and getting wealthy at the same time.

What was the reason for me going the proper way, working hard every day and then waking up in the morning so sore? I knew that if I acted like they did, others would call me out right away; certain people can get away with evil and others can't.

I even went to the sanctuary and prayed about this contrasting behavior. I then realized that we are aware of what these people are like, and that the day will come when they will fall, and that the last laugh belongs to us.

I then began to realize that the way I acted was also wrong. The envy created bitterness in my heart, tearing me up.

I prayed, "I am embarrassed to admit that I acted stupidly in front of you God, like a dumb animal, but I never stopped believing in you. I need you to walk with me through this life, holding my hand so to speak, until I am with you forever. There is no one in Heaven or earth like you. My strength and energy will weaken over time, but God will forever be strong in my heart. People don't accept that those who turn away from you will perish, the fate of all who don't believe. Oh, how glad I am to be with God and in your protective care! I'll tell others about you all my days.[148]Oh, forgive me for envying the proud."

The hand upon my shoulder surprised me, but I knew when Jesus said "Peace be with you" that I was forgiven, once again.

Day 13 – Children

Today we continued our discussion of children. I was expecting a light-hearted talk about childish habits, but that was not the topic that Jesus wanted to impress on me. In fact, Jesus was disheartened that many people don't appreciate children, forgetting that they began that way themselves.

"God has always treasured children, and the Scriptures speak of this love," Jesus said. "In fact, he has instructed couples to have many children,[149] calling each a gift and blessing.

"Women, instinctively, have always been saddened when they weren't permitted to bear children.[150] They understood that a blessing came through childbirth.[151] Often the Lord has blessed childless women by allowing them to bear children; when others were not allowed, it was because the time was not right or that God had a different purpose for them."

"Parents, naturally, are always to care for their children and to love them," I said. But Jesus already knew my thoughts: that the things he was saying were common knowledge.

"There are many things that have been written that should be practiced, but man disregards so much that is good for him," Jesus answered. "Even regarding children."

Then Jesus made me cringe when he reminded me about the detestable practice that occurred throughout the centuries: children being sacrificed to idols—false gods.[152] "Children have suffered through all ages and for many reasons; this greatly angers God.[153]"

"I heard about the horrible sacrificing of children to Molech. I didn't understand how a parent could do that," I commented.

"This also saddened God," Jesus said, "because He knew them from the beginning, He formed them in the womb, He gave them life—but this fact is ignored."[154]

"Even though sacrificing to Molech doesn't happen now," Jesus continued, "children are still sacrificed. If parents only realized that God had plans for their children even before they were formed,[155] would they still end the life of a little one? People try to take control for themselves, taking control away from God, and judging for themselves if a newly created life is to continue—sometimes even waiting until after the birth of the child. The love a mother normally has for her child is covered and blocked. These children that God gave life to will have life taken away for the sake of other gods."

"Other than Molech, what gods are these?" I asked.

"There are many, common gods such as the god of selfishness or because of the result of the god of pleasure." "Don't they realize that they should never," and Jesus told me how he made this point clear to the disciples, saying plainly, "*never* despise a single one of these little ones? For I tell you that they have angels who see my Father's face continually in Heaven."[156]

Jesus said that the mothers who end their children's lives should feel great remorse at this. He said that his "Father in Heaven is not willing that any of these little ones should be lost."[157] But he assured me that all people are sinful, and that they too can be forgiven, all sins can be forgiven,[158] if they come to him asking and confessing.

Jesus was passionate about this subject, so this afternoon I was taught what was contained in the ancient Scriptures about children. Jesus talked about how God created man and woman to love and worship him and He would love them as his children; we would be called children of God.[159] He didn't create the world and then desire it to remain empty, but full of people whom He loved. He wants to watch over us and protect us, and He has a plan for each of us.

We are to do the same for our children. We are to take care of them, and just as the Father teaches us, we are to instruct our children. God instructed *us* to teach them: teach them His words, teach them at all times, no matter where we are or what we're doing.[160] This command is for the parents themselves, not someone else; the parents are to teach their children. God instructed us, "Teach them to *your* children." [161] Even God teaches His own people, His children.[162] This is what the Father desires.

Sometimes, children don't listen—by definition they are still young and still learning—so they must be set in the right direction. A parent does this to protect them from more serious harm at a later time. Sometimes the correction is painful. Does a parent really love a child if he doesn't correct him? It might seem harsh for the parent to discipline, but the child will be better for it. The Father does that to his children as well.[163] He has stated, "I correct and discipline everyone I love."[164]

Then Jesus smiled. "There is more proof of the importance God places on children, and this was most significant,"...and then Jesus paused and looked at me to see if I knew. "He sent his Son to reconcile his people not as a man, already grown up, but as a child, and in a very unique way at that; it also fulfilled scripture.[165]

He had one more comment on the subject, saying: "I wish people would accept what God commanded for mankind's own good: 'Have plenty of children. Fill the earth and rule it.'"[166]

We sat quietly for awhile, and I pondered all that Jesus had said. Then a question occurred to me. I hesitated and then cautiously asked, "But what about Daniel? How does he fit in? He is so different from the people of the world. I love him dearly. Can he be healed to be like everyone else?"

Then Jesus filled my mind with understanding that I had never considered before. He instructed me to seriously consider what I was asking.

Jesus repeated my question. "Can he be healed?" Then Jesus inquired if Daniel really needed healing.

I said that he was different from everyone else. "When we go to the market place people stare at him. I can see them wondering what is wrong with him, why he is so different."

Jesus said they looked at him differently too. Many were afraid of him, even wanting to kill him.

Jesus then said, "We should take a closer look at this situation. I've been watching over him a long time, from the very beginning. You are very fortunate. He is physically well, he loves unconditionally, asks for forgiveness when he does do wrong, doesn't hold anger towards anyone, is unashamed about showing his love to others and he is a gentle person. He is of good disposition: he's happy and enjoys life. The simple pleasures bring joy to him. He also trusts and loves you completely as you should trust God—the faith of a child."

Then we talked about the things Daniel doesn't do. "He doesn't devise plans or plot to do evil. He isn't arrogant. He doesn't lie. He doesn't associate with people who stir up trouble and he doesn't do harm to others," Jesus said. That's when I realized that Jesus really does know Daniel.

Jesus then turned to the things that are required of me because Daniel is different. "Daniel gives you as a parent the opportunity to show love unconditionally to someone in spite of their perceived flaws or differences. This is a good practice that helps you become a good example to others.

"Because he is different and you don't have answers to why he is different and why he was given to you, you must yourself trust God with the question of 'why'. Think about that: Daniel's existence helps you to trust God. That's a good result too."

"You asked about healing him. If he was made to be like everyone else on earth, you would no longer recognize him. He would be someone else, not Daniel."

Then Jesus leaned over and looked at me with eyes that penetrated to my very soul. With utmost compassion, he said, "You are to trust the paths that the Father leads you on, though you might not understand why. He told Jeremiah something long ago and His words will always remain true. He said, "For I know the plans I have for you, plans to prosper you and not to harm you, plans to give you hope and a future."[167]

Then looking at Daniel, still playing in the field, Jesus opened his arms and said, "Anyone who welcomes a little child like this on my behalf welcomes me, and anyone who welcomes me also welcomes my Father who sent me. Whoever is the least among you is the greatest."[168]

Daniel among the greatest; I am so humbled to be his father.

Day 15 – Divine

Jesus instructed me to write down the events of the days before his resurrection from the dead. He said it had already been written down but he wanted another record of it for a different people at a different time. Many others would put in writing the events of those incredible days, men who had been in Jerusalem and were observers to all he endured. Those reminisces would be read by numerous people, as many as there are stars in the sky. I wasn't privileged to know how many would read my text.

It seems so clear, now that it has been explained to me, but I'm writing after the events happened and I have been privileged to witness the Christ, the living Son of God. That he suffered those final days was evident by the many scars and by the holes in his feet and hands. Who wouldn't be able to easily believe when the scars are right before them?

Jesus began by telling me that he had met resistance from his own people since he was young. Some had received visions that he would appear, but many others would not believe: the religious leaders, other Jews, his own people. They did not want to believe even though their own Scriptures spoke of him. He healed many sick people and even gave back life to some who died. This should have convinced them of who he was, where he got his power and who his Father was that he spoke of, but they even ignored the miracles.

When he went from town to town, the ones who did believe were those who sincerely repented and knew how lost and helpless they were.

He explained that his ancestor was David, the ancient king of Israel who found favor from God. David had written about him so many years before, but many people's hearts were hardened and they could not believe.

He was not born to people who were rich and privileged or of high position or royalty. He had to start at the bottom, just as a new plant begins by breaking through the dry ground, alone and unimportant, without fanfare and celebration.

"One person announced my arrival," Jesus said. "A man called John. He taught in the wild, outside of the towns. He preached for everyone to turn from their sinful ways and he baptized those who sincerely repented. People don't easily turn from their sinful ways, not without God's help. John also told the people I was coming soon."

Jesus continued his account, telling how it filled him with great sorrow to see the people hungry or ill or grieving. But some towns forbade his entering, and once he was almost thrown from a cliff. But the holy angels protected him; it was not yet time for his suffering.

The message he delivered was not appealing to people. Those teaching at the temple thought he was blaspheming God, but how could he blaspheme himself or be disrespectful to his Father? His message was so resisted that it caused people to turn away from him as if he was repulsive to look at. There were people who should have known better, but they wouldn't acknowledge who he was. In fact, they thought he was unimportant and insignificant.

Jesus then related some of the awful suffering he endured those last days. Evil forces had their way; they struck him and hit him and mocked him. They thought he was getting what he deserved. They reasoned that his punishment was from God, that this was justice being carried out, confirming his guilt.

They drove spikes through his hands and feet, nailing him to a cross. Later a soldier thrust his spear, piercing his side and fatally wounding him. People didn't realize he was enduring what *they* deserved. He was a substitute for the suffering that we all deserve for our sinful ways, but the people saw it the opposite way.

Jesus then explained that this was his purpose. He was sent to reconcile us, to cleanse us, to make us presentable to God. This was the only way. He made peace between us and God. People are full of sin, the same as a disease, and Jesus has now healed us: he has saved us.

I asked Jesus, "*Who* was filled with sin? Who was healed?"

He replied, "Everyone is full of sin—all of mankind. But anyone who believes is saved. People are like your sheep out in that field. Remember when the earth quaked? The sheep ran off in different directions. They ran away from their shepherd. Each turned and went its own direction; they followed their own will. People are like that also, they have always been that way. They turn away from God and go their own sinful way. To make peace with His people, God dropped all the sins of all people on me, His Son, and I suffered for everyone."

"How could you be found guilty? Was there a trial first? Did you defend yourself? Did you speak out and say you were innocent? I have seen the Roman soldiers arrest people and I know they can be brutal. Were they rough on you also?" I asked.

Jesus responded, "I *was* treated cruelly and there was a trial, so to speak, but it was done very quickly."

Jesus said he didn't defend himself; he kept silent, for that was God's desire. To carry out redemption, he could not contest the charges. He wasn't guilty, but he was going to be punished as if he *was* guilty. Even though the people had laws, they neglected their own methods to carry out his crucifixion.

When their proceedings were done, and Pilate, the governor, had judged that the crucifixion would be allowed, the process for Jesus' death was put into action. He was made to carry his own cross to Golgotha, after he had been beaten and whipped and thorny vines were twisted together as a mock crown and crushed onto his head. He went willingly, without a fight; just like sheep when they are to be sheared, or to be slaughtered, he was silent as he went to be crucified.

"Why didn't the people protest?" I asked.

"This generation doesn't comprehend." He said they didn't understand that he wasn't dying for his own misdeeds—*his* sins—of which he has none, but for the sins of all people.

The wrenching ordeal of the crucifixion is hard to stomach. It leaves the body disfigured and severely damaged. Most people have trouble even looking at the cross.

Normally, when it is finished, the body would be cast outside the town with the others who had received the same punishment. (Crucified alongside Jesus were men who *had* committed crimes.) But a good man stepped forward, an honorable man named Joseph, who arranged for Jesus' body to be buried respectfully in a tomb that was originally carved out to be his own.

Being a parent, it is hard for me to comprehend what Jesus said next. "God is pleased that my suffering occurred. My death was a trespass offering: a final offering to pay, restitution for the sins of all people. God was satisfied that it was now completed. The substitution for sins was complete."

However, death was not the end. For in a few days he left the tomb (as I am so fortunate to know personally). His days will continue forever.

Jesus is also pleased that all who believe can now be at peace with God. They have become righteous and Satan has lost. Satan is no longer strong enough; Jesus paid the price for their souls. Now he will be exalted; he will take his place alongside God, his Father.

I asked, "Will people know what has been done for them, so they can believe?"

"All people will come to know about me, even those who weren't expecting me," Jesus replied. "They will be told, it will become obvious to them and they will believe. Even kings will be astonished and will bow down to me.[169]

"So not just the Jews?" I asked.

"*All* people,"[170] Jesus replied.

Jesus now reminded me of what he had said at the onset: this retelling of events—his crucifixion on the cross—had already been faithfully recorded. I was surprised because it had only happened a few weeks ago.

"Who has already written about these events?" I asked him.

He already knew my questioning thoughts (in truth, he knew them even before I thought them), but he patiently replied that it was Isaiah.[171]

"Isaiah!" I blurted out. "But he lived more than 700 years ago."

He agreed, and I asked another question.

"Which part of the crucifixion story did he foretell?"

His answer surprised me: "All of it. Isaiah was quite thorough."

Almost two weeks had passed since Jesus had opened my eyes to the many references in the old Scriptures which told of his coming. There were many other references which gave detailed accounts of the suffering he was to endure. He didn't want to discuss his suffering at that time. He wanted the other prophecies to also have importance; the ones that were written to describe that he was sent by God himself, that he was God's anointed from the beginning.

But today Jesus revealed to me what the prophet Isaiah had described, the recent week in Jerusalem, as if he had been here to witness the event. How could Isaiah know? How could he know 700 years before Jesus was even born? No one could imagine that the Savior, the Christ, would come to redeem his people and then be killed. Only one explanation is possible: the Spirit of God was at work in Isaiah to reveal to us God's magnificent plan.

"Was this foretold in other parts of the Scriptures too?" I asked.

"It was written about quite often," he replied.

Then Jesus began to tell me about many of these instances. He mentioned that the angel Gabriel, who has been given the privilege of making many important announcements, gave Daniel advance knowledge of when he was to appear. Daniel called Jesus The Anointed One. He even specified the number of years after the temple was rebuilt until these recent events. Gabriel informed Daniel, and he faithfully recorded that the Savior would be killed and the purpose in being sacrificed would not be recognized[172]—the same as Isaiah had been inspired to write.

Zechariah declared that he would be of the family line of David and that they would pierce him; he wrote that they would look at him as one who is on display while being pierced.[173]

Jesus then pointed out that David had mentioned him many times, and said that his death would be by crucifixion (that they would pierce his hands and feet[174] and then gamble for his clothes[175]), which the Roman soldiers did before his very eyes.[176] David wrote that while Jesus was hanging on the cross, suffering, they would mock and ridicule him, saying "Why doesn't he save himself?"[177] He even described the evil fascination of the spectators, how they stared and gloated at Jesus while watching him die.[178] And lastly, David even recorded Jesus' final words.[179]

To end the crucifixion, the Romans always break the bones of those they have nailed up, but Jesus' bones were not broken; David wrote about this detail as well.[180] (I have to remind myself that David lived a thousand years before all of this happened.)

"Even the prophet Amos mentioned the events that you experienced."

"Me?"

"Yes, he wrote: 'In that day, I will make the sun go down at noon and darken the earth in broad daylight.'"[181]

"Yes, I remember it well."

Jesus continued to describe the many times the Scriptures had mentioned the details of his death. It was hard to believe so much could be written so long ago about the events that had just taken place. Even though first written 400 to 1,000 or more years ago, they sound like they were written by actual witnesses. I guess that's why they're called prophets.

Someone who proclaims lies is not a prophet but a fraud. How does one profess events that actually *do* occur—events that in time prove factual? Where does the inspiration come from to not only predict the coming of the Son of God, but something as extraordinary as the crucifixion of the Son of God? Of course, the inspiration must have come from God. The Spirit of God was at work in these people, these prophets.

I'll restate what I said earlier that now is so clear. Jesus was crucified. He died on the cross, just as Isaiah and David and Daniel and many others wrote so long ago. What was written applies to the one who is with me now. He was killed, but Jesus has risen from the dead. He is very much alive.

The Scriptures are true; they can be believed and trusted. That cannot be denied.

Day 16 – Forgive

I spent today recording Jesus' latest teachings on the scrolls. When he left last night, Jesus mentioned a special breakfast he planned for today; He would be having fish with his disciples. They had finally followed his instructions and gone to Galilee, which he had directed them to do both before and after leaving the tomb.

At the end of the day, I found fish being cooked over a fire again, a sign that Jesus had met with the disciples. This time, he was staying to have his meal with us.

I asked if the disciples caught many fish; it brought quite a laugh in response. Jesus said, "They had more than they knew what to do with—but the nets didn't break.[182] Peter wasn't much help to his fellow fishermen. He jumped out of the boat and swam to greet me at shore, leaving the others to pull in the nets."

Peter was the one Jesus wanted to talk to, anyways. Jesus explained that Peter was very boastful. To be a servant, a good servant, he would need to be humbled, but not broken. On Jesus' last night with the disciples (the night before the crucifixion), Peter brashly stated that he would never deny him. In fact, he boasted that he would die for him.[183]

Well, later that night on three occasions, Peter denied that he had any association with Jesus—in fact, he denied that he even knew Jesus.[184] Jesus, who knows everything, even before it happens, had specifically warned Peter that this would happen.[185]

After the crucifixion, Peter was one of the first people to see Jesus after he arose from the tomb, but there was a hole in the relationship that needed to be patched. It was like two layers of cloth with a hole through both layers. Jesus had forgiven everyone, so his side of the cloth was fixed, but now Peter had to come to accept that his side also needed to be repaired.

To do that, Jesus had commanded that the disciples go to Galilee. He had told them this before he died and after he had risen; eventually they did go there. It was quite a distance from Jerusalem to Galilee, but going there placed Peter in the comfortable surroundings of his home. Peter was especially at ease in his boat in the Sea of Galilee, so that is how Jesus went to Peter. He explained that he sought out Peter (and that he goes to each person seeking them).

As they ate their breakfast, Jesus talked to Peter and proceeded to fill in the hole that his denials had created. Jesus knew that Peter had great remorse for denouncing him, especially since it had been foretold. Peter's burden was even more overwhelming to him once he became aware that Jesus knew about the denials. He felt that once again he had disappointed Jesus, who had such high expectations for him.

Jesus explained that no one is able to reach the standards that God has set for perfection. No one is perfect except God, but that is why Jesus came to us, to bridge this gap between man's falseness and God's holiness. We are only able to accomplish this through Jesus; he is the way to God.

Jesus had great plans for Peter. But first Peter needed to publicly acknowledge Jesus in order to repair the damage of his three public denials and also the damage to their relationship. To do this, Jesus said he asked Peter three times if he loved him, and Peter affirmed that he did. Peter's forgiveness was now complete in Peter's eyes. The confession was simple, but Jesus said he doesn't demand something difficult from us, or place a heavy weight upon us—what he asks of

us is easy and doesn't weigh us down with many require-
ments.[186]

So Peter finally learned the miracle of forgiveness. He
denied the Savior of the world, with whom he had been constantly for three years, but was now forgiven. Jesus explained
that Peter would also need to forgive just as he had been forgiven. The great plans Jesus had for him would require Peter
to forgive those who had shouted for his crucifixion. Peter
would no longer deny Jesus, but instead stand boldly pro-
claiming his faith, and by standing strong, convince people
throughout many lands to repent and believe.

Jesus further explained that forgiveness had always been
one of the keys of his teachings. God gave him the authority
on earth to forgive sins.[187] We are also to forgive those who
have offended us and hopefully they will forgive us when we
offend them, for we (all the people of God's creation) are a
sinful people. The act of forgiveness by Jesus was completed
fully when he died on the cross, paying our debt for all time.
We are forgiven when we come to him, confessing our sins.
But we are also wrong if we think we have not sinned. If we
think we have no sin, then we don't need Jesus.

Peter had trouble with forgiveness; he needed to receive
forgiveness so that he could understand the needs of others
and thus have compassion. Jesus said that Peter would often
become frustrated when people continued to err, and would
ask in exasperation: "How many times shall I forgive my
brother when he sins against me?"[188] Jesus would tell him
there was no limit on forgiveness.

"Peter has now learned," Jesus said, "and he'll be a solid
example for the church to build on. Satan won't be able to
destroy it."[189]

Many people put themselves up on a pedestal so they can
look down on certain people, or just look down on everyone.

They have difficulty learning about forgiveness. They reason that they have no faults within them, no sin, and they're glad they're not like their neighbor. I must admit, that I, the one who is writing this, have been guilty of this also. I have asked for, and received, forgiveness of this sin. Jesus pointed out to me that when those who have sinned greatly receive forgiveness (which is also a great amount), the joy, thankfulness and outward love they show to others is also great.[190]

Jesus made sure I also recorded that he went to Peter at Peter's home where he lived and was comfortable. Peter didn't seek Jesus. Jesus reached out to Peter as he reaches out to everyone, as if he was standing on our door step knocking on the door.[191] It is then up to us to open the door and let Jesus into our lives, which he will surely do. Many won't open the door. Forgiveness of sins and life eternal with God will remain closed to them and they will not be saved. But many will open the door and welcome him in.

Jesus said that Peter and his fellow fishermen, the apostles, will have an important role in bringing this message to the world. Jesus instructed them to return to Jerusalem where he'll see them a few more times before he returns to his Father. Repentance and forgiveness of sins will be preached to all nations, but it will begin in Jerusalem.[192]

It was now getting late. The fish had been gone for quite awhile and the fire needed more wood to keep burning. Jesus said he was going to go and talk to his Father for a while. He had more for me to record on the scrolls, and inquired if I had enough ink. He smiled when I replied that the level in the ink jar never changed, no matter how much I wrote. I also commented that the quills were very strong, unlike any I had ever used.

He then walked over to Daniel, gave him a big hug, and gave us a blessing for a restful night.

Day 18 – As a Child

Once again I watched over the flock, this time walking around the lush grazing field looking for anything that might be harmful to the ewes. But this site was as ideal as one could imagine. There was nothing to be worried about. The main concern now is keeping an eye on Daniel so that he doesn't wander away. He is easily distracted when he doesn't have a definite task before him, and this location does not demand much attention. The sheep are content and move only a short distance throughout the day.

There is one attraction that insures that Daniel does stay nearby, and that is Jesus. Daniel loves him and always sits near him when he comes to our protected area—our temporary home at the foot of the stairway which leads to Heaven—and listen to him as he talks to us.

Daniel doesn't always understand what we are discussing but there is one thing he does understand: trust. Daniel completely trusts Jesus. He doesn't find it necessary to understand everything; he just knows that, being in Jesus' presence, there is nothing to fear. Everyone should have such confidence, Jesus would point out.

Many times, by the time a conversation is over, Daniel has fallen asleep at Jesus' feet. He'll be totally at peace—like a small child sleeping in his parent's arms—with nothing to fear.[193]

Usually Daniel is quiet, but this time he suddenly asked "You really feed thousands?"

"Yes, certainly I did; many times. Which time do you mean?"

"Boy with fish and loaves."[194]

"Who told you about this?"

"My friend."

"Was this when you were at the market before this journey?" Jesus asked. By the way he said it, I knew that Jesus knew the answer—as if he had seen them talking.[195]

"Yes." He answered, nodding his head. "By the grapes."

Then Jesus told him about the day he fed five thousand men and their families with only five loaves of bread and two fish.

"It must have been big loaves and big fish."

Jesus laughed and told him that both the fish and bread were quite small.

"How you do it?" Daniel asked. I wondered as well, but I knew anything was possible for God.[196]

"I prayed. Then I just kept handing them out to the disciples and they kept handing them out to the people. When everyone was done, we just put the leftovers back in some baskets."[197]

"Leftovers?" Daniel asked.

"From five loaves and two fish?" I questioned.

"Twelve baskets—*full*," Jesus stated.

Daniel and I both sat there marveling at the miracle Jesus performed for those people. God's power was demonstrated right before their eyes.

Then Jesus explained, "Many people weren't convinced about who I was, even though I often did extraordinary things. The miracles were done as proof that the Father and I are one. They were done openly, too, but the people were slow to believe. People have always been stubborn about believing and trusting in God.

"Like this time with the bread and the fish, God has used food throughout the years as a method to prove his existence. I know you heard many times about the manna and the quail in the desert when Israel left Egypt, [198] and that was 600,000 men and their families.[199] Remember, that lasted for 40 years,"[200] Jesus added.

"Do you remember that Elijah was given food when he fled Ahab and Jezebel?[201] He was served bread and meat, morning and night, by ravens. That food was provided by God, of course...or do *you* know of any birds that prepare food?"[202]

Jesus smiled, and then continued.

"After this, Elijah was again served food in a unique way by a widow in the town of Zarephath.[203] She prepared food from a jar of oil and a jar of flour that she never refilled. Yet they never failed to feed her and her son, much less Elijah. Where did that come from?

"God even provided a well of water in the desert to quench the thirst of Hagar and her son, the servant of Sarah, Abraham's wife.[204] I recently fed the disciples fish on the shore of the Sea of Galilee and I have also fed you.

"God has fed people in very visible ways, many times over the years. This is so they can learn not to doubt where their nourishment is coming from and that he does love his people and promises to take care of them. Only a few of the times, however, has this been recorded on scrolls; don't think those are the only times this happened.

"But don't overlook larger ways also; unfortunately, people don't comprehend the source behind them."

"What do you mean?" I asked.

"When the storms blow in, and the fields are watered, do you ever consider that that may be from God too? Do you think that every year when the rivers fill and water the fields that it is by chance?[205] Do you really think the seasons just happen also: year after year, the same sequence as the previous year? God is a God of order and the order is for your benefit. This order is visible everywhere: from plants and animals, fish and seas, to seasons and the stars and moons to the farthest distances.[206] Everything is under his control.

"God is also a God who watches over his people, and He hears their prayers. When I taught people about God's protective care, I specifically preached not to worry about where your food or drink will come from. Those sheep over in that field and the birds flying around us, they aren't concerned but they have what they need. Aren't you far more valuable to God than they are?[207] Food and drink are important, but they are not the most important thing. Put your energy into having faith in God. Believe in me, his Son and my being the path to salvation. Be concerned about God's kingdom first and he will provide what you need.[208] Trust in God."

Daniel was smiling now, but he was also looking at his stomach and rubbing it.

"Too much talk about food?" Jesus asked him. "But you aren't worried, are you?"

Daniel shook his head.

"Faith of a child—be like that. Put your trust in the One who is in charge of everything and accept God's protective care."[209]

Day   20   –   Rules

Jesus surprised me today. Rather, I was unaware of his presence.

I was busy explaining to Daniel that I wanted him to inspect the fields, look after the sheep and check for insects on their face and bodies, and do a few other things— including keeping himself clean. I was trying to be patient but at the same time getting a little exasperated with the process.

I have been through this many times before. I reminded myself that Daniel is different, he is not like me. He needs repeated instructions to carry out the tasks that I require, which are not meaningless; they have a purpose. They protect the sheep and him from harm and illness. Today I found him not wearing his shepherd's scrip, his small leather bag for carrying important items including his sling and some stones. A few days ago I had him look for some nice smooth stones in the stream that skirts this grazing field. I had stressed that if some wild animal threatened the sheep, he would need the stones.

All these details seem small, but the business of shepherding is more enjoyable and fulfilling when the proper methods are followed. It will also be more successful: the herd survives, and in the end, more wool is sheared to bring to the market.

Yes, I have told him all this before—many times before, and I also realize that everything I tell him today will have to be repeated on another day. Will this cycle never end? Can't he just comprehend what is for his good, and also mine and the sheep's own well-being? I should realize that the harder I try to instruct him, the more my patience decreases, and then he withdraws and absorbs even less.

This is when Jesus made his presence known to me. He walked up to me from behind. I should have heard his sandals as he stepped on the sticks and gravel, but I was so involved in my thoughts that I jumped when he placed his hand on my shoulder.

"Can't comprehend what is good." Jesus asked—or was he stating? Was he observing the difficulty I was having or was he reading my thoughts?

"If I've told him once I've told him a thousand times…" I began, but I didn't finish my sentence. Jesus was nodding in agreement, but he wasn't looking at Daniel. He was looking at *me*.

"I meant…I was talking…about Daniel."

Jesus paused and then said: "Yes, him too."

Him too? Him too? What did he mean? I was afraid to know.

"There are many rules in life," Jesus said.

"I agree," I said. "A father or mother has many things to teach their children when they're young. As they get older, others will teach them too. When they learn a trade they'll have even more rules to remember."

"Some rules are more important than others—some will save your life."[210]

"I often warn Daniel about the danger of certain herbs. He even still gets careless around fire."

"Yes, the fire."

"I'm always careful to put out the fire when I can't keep a close eye on it and Daniel."

"It never will go out," Jesus said.[211]

I almost said that I put water on the fire to make sure it's extinguished, but then I realized that Jesus was talking about something more important than my rules and a little camp-fire.

"Rules and fire, ignore the one and the result is the other. Rules or laws, call them commands, they *are* good for you and they make life easier for you. Ignore them and you will be destroyed." [212]

"What rules are those that are so dangerous? I asked.

"God's rules," Jesus replied. "He has said what He expects."

I now understood that Jesus was referring to the ancient laws and commands. I remember my teachers spending an extensive amount of time on this. I haven't killed anyone and I've always been faithful to Meira, my wife. I believe I've followed the other laws as well, so I shouldn't have anything to be concerned about. These thoughts were in my head, but I became uncomfortable just the same. Jesus was very serious now. He knew every moment of my past; could I be so sure that I was innocent? No, I couldn't.

Then my heart sank as Jesus said: "Everyone looks the other way, everyone is corrupt; there is no one who does good, not even a single person."[213]

Here I've been, relaxing in this beautiful location, instructing my son in rules he should obey, and not realizing that there is a storehouse of rules and commands—for me and from God—that I have ignored, forgotten, twisted to my convenience, determined that they don't apply to me, decided they were out of date, accepted because everyone else did, were silly, were too hard…and countless other reasons. Have I been guilty my entire life? I guess I have been.

I have made myself a judge of God's laws. Who am I to do that? Oh, am I that sinful? Yes.

Then I had a thought—a way out. Jesus said that we only have to believe in him to be saved. Maybe the old rules don't have to be followed.

So I asked: "Since you came to save us, do the laws still apply?"

"Yes, they still do apply," Jesus answered. "Don't think that I have come to abolish the laws given to Moses or the writings of the prophets; I have not come to abolish them but to fulfill them."[214]

My knees began to buckle as my despair increased—so I sat down on a nearby rock. Even though it was still cool this morning, sweat began to cover my face.

Then Jesus said even more. "You have heard it said many times 'do not murder, do not commit adultery, don't break your oaths, it's permissible to divorce, an eye for an eye,' and all the other things.

"Yes, I have listened to those instructions from when I was very young."

"Well, those rules are not strong enough. Don't even be angry at someone. Don't even swear an oath to ensure you do something, do good to everyone—even your enemy. It is not enough to satisfy God by what you do, what matters is what is in your heart. And understand this: unless you follow all God's rules to the smallest detail you cannot get into the kingdom of God."[215]

I had no answer to this—I was guilty.

"God takes this very seriously, Shemaiah." Jesus said.

I leaned over, looking down at the dirt, and placed my head in my hands. Jesus didn't say any more. He patted me on the back; when I eventually looked up, he was gone.

Daniel had seen my distress and was now sitting by my side, so I put my arm around him and told him how sorry I was for being rough on him earlier. Daniel is always very forgiving; my apology was accepted.

We tended to the sheep for the remainder of the day. I didn't offer much further conversation to Daniel this day. When darkness came, I was too ashamed to climb the ridge, so we turned in early.

I lay down on my bedroll but sleep didn't come easily. There was no comfortable position; whenever my eyes did close in sleep, I was soon startled awake with horrible dreams.

I wished there was a place to hide, but I knew there was no place I could go.[216] Was my destiny to feel the flames of the fire Jesus mentioned? The fire whose flames will never go out?

Tomorrow is the Sabbath. Just as well. I don't think I will have the desire to carry out any tasks anyways.

I can't do it. I can't get to the holy kingdom. I have sinned too much.

Day 22 – Saved

The sun came up earlier than usual today—at least it seemed that way. Having tossed and turned for a second night, and unable to relax, my joints and muscles were very sore. I rolled over and slowly forced my legs to make my body stand. I reasoned that I must have aged 20 years these last two nights.

I leaned against the wall of rocks, the wall that we climb to see the Golden Stairway, and Jesus' words that he often repeated kept going through my head: "All you have to do to be saved, to have eternal life, is to believe in God's Son." But he also said, "Unless you follow all God's rules to the smallest detail you cannot get into the kingdom of God."

I am so confused.

As I began to ready myself for the day, a pleasant aroma caught my attention. I walked into the clearing and there I found Jesus, sitting on some rocks in the bright sun, grilling cakes over a small fire; a special treat.

"Peace be with you this beautiful day that my Father has provided."

I bowed and greeted Jesus also and then commented that the smell of the cakes was better than fine perfume. He informed me that it was an old recipe.

He then told me to wake Daniel, for the meal was almost ready.

The food and friendly conversation lifted my spirit, but Jesus knew what was still in my thoughts. He waited for me to ask.

Finally, I said: "But didn't you say that all I have to do to be saved, to have eternal life, is believe you are God's Son?"

"Yes.[217] Why were you so worried? I already forgave your sins. You have been saved from death. You knew that. I don't save you then 'un-save' you. Be assured, I'll never leave you, unless of course you decide to leave me."[218]

"But what about all those laws?" I asked.

"They are for people who don't believe in God's Son as the way to receive salvation. They can try to save themselves by pleasing God, but that means following the smallest letter of the law.

"But that's impossible," I said.

"You are correct. People think they can save themselves by what they do, but they can't. No one can save themselves. Their actions reveal their belief that I am a liar, but they are very mistaken; I am the only way.

"The agony you were experiencing, Shemaiah, because you were realizing how sinful you are, should be felt by all. They need to believe too—but sadly only a few do."

"Do the laws given to Moses still have a purpose?" I asked. And then Jesus patiently explained to me how the old rules and laws fit in with God's plan of man's salvation through His Son. At first it seemed complicated, but eventually I was able to see the meaning plainly.

The law shows us our sins—how sinful we are—that we have nowhere to go to be saved from our sinfulness except to Jesus. I realized myself when I reflected on my old sinful ways (and also my current sinful ways) that I had failed to meet God's standard. His standard is perfection; no one on earth has ever done that except for Jesus. This perfection not only applies to what we do, but also to what we think. This standard leaves no one who is qualified.

If we didn't have God's laws, we wouldn't recognize how deplorable we really are, and we wouldn't go to Jesus. Because of the laws, we learn that we have failed. God delights in those who recognize their failure[219] and turn to him. Furthermore, He doesn't rebuke them when they seek Him either; he just forgives.[220] We should be thankful that God really does care for His creation and doesn't wish that anyone be lost—that anyone not be able to enter His Kingdom.[221]

As we talked, Jesus identified the source of our sinful behavior: Satan. Satan has been very successful at his work of bringing us down. The reason Jesus came was to destroy the works of the devil.[222] He came to free us from this prison, this bondage to sin,[223] but if we deny Jesus and fail to confess that we are sinful we remain prisoners, and do not receive the spiritual freedom Jesus offers.

God takes this all seriously. That is why he sent His Son[224] to save us from our sinful ways. But if we feel our sins aren't real, then Jesus isn't a real savior to us.[225] And we shouldn't think that Jesus is only capable of forgiving small sins—then we make Jesus small. Do we think our sins are so great that not even Jesus can forgive us? Then we make Jesus out to be a liar.

When we were discussing the size of sins Jesus said there are sins that aren't forgiven, very large ones and small sins, too.

"What sins are these?" I asked.

"The sins committed by someone not concerned with God."

When he said this, I felt a great sadness. I couldn't understand why anyone would want to deny God and remain in the devil's grasp. Somehow they must be comfortable being separated from God. I remembered Jesus' comment about the fire that never goes out; I don't think they'll always feel comfortable.

"So do God's laws apply to those who are saved?" I asked.

"Yes, they still apply," Jesus said. "Follow God's laws out of love for Him. God created everything and He's a God of order. If He can order the planets, don't you think He also has a plan for man? You'll find it's the best way to live your life."

Tonight, Daniel and I climbed the ridge to view Jesus in his glorious splendor. We are so privileged—and I don't mean just us two shepherds, but all people.

We watched for a while and then returned to our sheep-fold and camp to settle in for the night. Having had a couple of nights of fitful slumber, I looked forward to a restful sleep, knowing that my eternal destination is secure.

Day 24 – Peace

Since finding myself at the foot of the stairway that leads to Heaven, I wake up each morning with the anticipation of being with Jesus and learning about God's desires for mankind. This has made every sunrise a joy to experience, and I embrace each new day. This joy continues throughout the day. The exhilarating experience of the morning is repeated at the end of the day when the sun lowers itself in the sky and disappears below the distant horizon, but not until it exits with a colorful display made more magnificent by the clouds in the sky.

Being with Jesus, the creator of everything including life, gives a person a confidence that is quite foreign, but very soothing and satisfying. When in his presence, the body releases all tension and anxiety, and his creative works and purpose can be enjoyed.

I like waking with this anticipation; it hasn't always been this way. Now I learn about God's plan and love for all people, but before this journey I struggled to rise each morning, wondering what God's plan is for just one person—that person being me.

I was reminiscing about this change of attitude today when Jesus approached me. Knowing my thoughts, he told me that I should have been asking him (praying to God) for wisdom[226] and comfort[227] and peace.[228]

We discussed this for a considerable amount of time. I confessed that I have had many days where my thoughts about past failures drag me down. I remember past endeavors that worked well for a length of time but then were not sustainable. I would attempt to go in a new direction without much success, or doors closed even before an attempt could be made. After a while, a heavy sadness would weigh me down. I struggled just to wake up in the morning, feeling like I had been flattened by a mill stone and needed to be scraped off.

I recounted how when I planted seeds and tried to grow crops, it rained too much or not enough. Disease or insects ruined the fruit on the vines. Even now, as I'm raising sheep for wool, sometimes predatory animals or illness diminish my flock. After so much time and strenuous work has been invested, I am barely able to carry on. Even recently, when the earth quaked and scattered my flock, at first I thought, "What more can happen?" But my sheep are slowly returning now. Maybe this time my loss will not be as severe.

Jesus understood the difficulties I was encountering, for he had lived as a man like me, too. He had watched his earthly father Joseph struggle to support his family as a carpenter. Sometimes there was work for him to do, sometimes there wasn't. Sometimes the wood he was working with would split, and his time invested was lost. He would have to start over or make a time-consuming repair. There were times he suffered an injury and couldn't work, and then when he was sick, again he wasn't able to work. When he died, the family struggled. Since Jesus was the oldest, he continued in his father's profession as a carpenter to provide for his mother and his siblings. He explained that when his ministry started three years ago, his brothers were old enough to take care of their mother.

"Unfortunately, the difficulties people face are related to sin entering the world," Jesus said, "beginning in God's beautiful garden at the creation. There are cherubim guarding it now,[229] and someday God may permit people to enter it again. But when that first couple disobeyed God, there were consequences and they had to be disciplined.

"Moses recorded what God said, writing poetically with the phrase: 'with the sweat of your brow' you will work the soil to produce food to eat.[230] But 'work the soil' meant all forms of work and all methods of providing for your needs. The soil in God's garden was pleasant to manage and productive; outside the garden, the ground would produce thorns and thistles and great effort would be needed to produce something different. All methods of providing for people's needs would become a struggle—it would become *work*. God was saying that because man went against His instructions, the way separate from God, the way He told him not to go, the direction Satan lead him—that he would have some hard work ahead of him; not only for him but for all his descendants as well. This couple's actions changed everything."

"You're talking about Adam and Eve, aren't you?"

"Of course. Even though they erred, they are good people. Immediately after they learned of the consequences and received their punishment, God promised to send a Savior to redeem them.[231] They had been enjoying very comfortable lives and were well-provided for in their first home, but they were tempted to desire more and they disobeyed God, so they were removed from the garden."

"With the hard work that came with independence, they also acquired anxiety and worry and death. They were very repentant and God always remained near them. He had walked with them and talked to them in the garden, so they had a relationship or bond with God. But as the years passed, most men did not believe. In fact, nearly all became evil[232] until there was only one who walked with God."[233]

" Noah?" I asked.

"Yes. There would be times when God provided extraordinary signs, usually through men who strongly believed. Many others would believe in God and trust him for awhile, but Satan would lure them away with his various tricks. But God always sustained the group of people who truly believed.[234]

"When men turn from God, they take upon themselves all of life's burdens, and troubles, and anxieties. Remember that we discussed previously how people reason that they are strong enough on their own, apart from God. They don't realize (at least not at first) that it is more than they can handle. God designed and desired man to walk with him; when they did, He blessed them.[235]

"God knew that man would not easily believe and walk with him until he saw proof. So from the beginning, God planned for someone to show people the way. Not just anyone would be sent, but his own Son, who is also God. For centuries, God has used many men to announce my eventual arrival."

Then Jesus explained that he has come now to show the way to God: he *is* that way. He said that God is not angry with us.[236] God loves his creation. That is why Jesus preached that we, weary and worn-out people, should cast off those worries that are weighing us down, take all our burdens, and turn them over to him—to Jesus, and he will give us peace and rest.[237] God has always promised rest to those who love Him.[238]

That's why we are not to worry; we don't *need* to worry. God provides for his people, and he knows what we need; just as he takes care of birds of the air, so does he take care of his people.[239] Worry has no power or strength to do anything helpful or good. Struggling all day to provide for your needs, from early in the day until late at night, worrying about what you will eat or what you will wear, shows that you are trusting in yourself to provide instead of trusting God.

"Have faith in God,"[240] Jesus said. "God does provide rest to his children, and sleep to those he loves."[241]

Jesus knows people suffer with great anguish, and he has seen it often these past years. "Bring these burdensome concerns to God for him to carry," he preached. "That is the way to find peace and rest."[242]

"How do we bring them to God?' I asked.

"Pray to God, talk to God, confide in Him your worries and fears, even your desires." [243] Jesus explained that he does that as well—he brings his concerns to his Father. He finds a secluded place, a private quiet place, and talks and listens to His Father in prayer.

Jesus leaned forward and looked into my eyes. With compassion, knowing how small and helpless I can be, He instructed me with the same words he said throughout his ministry: "If you have faith, faith in God, faith the amount of something as small as a little round seed,[244] then whatever you ask for in prayer"—and then he plainly said—"believe that you have received it, and it will be yours."[245]

"I can have whatever I want if I pray?" I asked.

"If it is in God's will."

"How do I know God's will?"

"You already know many of the things that God desires. One is to have faith in Him: faith that God knows what is best for you, faith that God provides what you need, faith that every good thing comes from God."

"Just believe it is going to be?" I said.

"Believe and ask that God's will would be done. If you don't believe, where is your faith?"

"Believe that God will answer my prayer," I said.

"God will provide what you need *at the proper time* so His purposes will be accomplished. Do you want what God *doesn't* desire for you?"

"No."

"People ask for something different every day. But God does hear and answer repeated prayers. Don't give up praying. Be persistent."[246]

"If it's in His will?" I asked again.

"Yes. God wants you to ask Him. Asking him shows where you put your faith. Asking him again places your thoughts on God as the source for the answer. It places your dependence in the proper place: on God. Understand your motives, confess your sins, don't hold anything against anyone else—forgive them—so that God may forgive you,[247] and humble yourself. God shows his grace to the humble—he lifts them up. He is not far away. If you turn to God, he will come close to you.[248] Remember, seek God's kingdom and seek to be in His will."[249]

"I can see you now," I said, "but what about when you aren't here, when I can't see you? Then it's not easy."

"When I go back to the Father I will send God's spirit to be with you,"[250] Jesus said, adding "and the Spirit will help you to pray.[251] By praying you can even move a mountain and throw it into the sea, if that is God's will. People have many mountains in their lives; God wants us to bring them to him in prayer."

Over the past few years, Jesus took his disciples with him to quiet places, teaching them by example to talk to his Father personally, teaching his disciples how to pray. Jesus then taught me. Here's what he taught me:

When we pray, speak respectively to our sacred Father, our God in Heaven, who created everything.

Pray that the sinful world may be replaced by His kingdom and His presence and what He desires.

Pray that He would provide what we need each day to survive and to forgive our sinful behavior. Since we are loved by God, and He freely forgives our faults, we should show love to our neighbors and forgive sins which they have committed against us.

Pray also that God will guide us in the proper paths, away from the directions that Satan entices and tricks us into doing. Jesus again emphasized that we should forgive others if we desire our Father to forgive us.[252]

Jesus also told me this: "Pray, but don't just babble on and on with endless and flowery words, especially just to show off lengthy prayers to others. When you pray, go into your room. Shut the door and pray in secret, for God knows what you need before you ask Him.[253] Be joyful and pray constantly, not just when faced with worry and anxiety, but give thanks in all circumstances, for this is God's will for you because of me, his Son."[254]

Our discussion of prayer continued for several hours, interspersed with examples of answered prayers, some even recorded in the Scriptures, and then Jesus departed. His time on earth when people would see him was limited and he needed to show his resurrected body to others.

I went into the field to help Daniel with the sheep and to play some simple games (Daniel loves games). I tired before Daniel did, so I went back to the big rock to do my work: writing on the scrolls.

I sat for a while contemplating this day's conversation, and became aware of a sense of happiness that filled me. I've been talking to God—Jesus—more than ever in my life and

I'm more at peace than ever in my life. Something to think about.

Day 25 – Success

So I was thinking again (this location allows a lot of time for thinking) about that first day I saw Jesus; I should say the first day that I talked to Jesus. He said he had *had* plans for me and then he told me to write and so I wrote. I recalled the proverb saying, "Trust in the LORD with all your heart and lean not on your own understanding," and then, "in all your ways acknowledge him, and he will make your paths straight."[255]

I do try to trust the Lord, but when things don't go as I planned, I wonder at which step I should have been trusting more and didn't that caused me to end up in a position I didn't desire. I don't mean here, on this ridge with Jesus, I mean in situations where my various pursuits have floundered. It sure would be refreshing to always have straight paths, as the proverb goes.

When I mentioned my past and my different attempts at providing for my family, Jesus said I should have prayed. I did pray some, but was it sincere or more of a curse of exasperation? I don't recall exactly—or maybe I don't recall because I'm afraid and embarrassed to admit that there was more "me" than God in my plans.

When I try to put this all together, it's confusing. I have failed at many endeavors, from planting seeds to tending vines to watching over sheep. If I would have prayed more, would one of these undertakings have been more profitable and made me wealthy? Maybe I would have had a large ranch or farm, or a beautiful vineyard that produced much sought-after wine. I could have had a large house and many servants to take care of all my needs: servants for the house and servants for the fields. I could have lived like a king or at least a lord.

I paused on this last word: "lord." What was I thinking? I only have one Lord: Jesus, my Savior. Yes, if I had all those things, I would be a lord unto myself. My thoughts would have all been directed towards me: *my* pleasures, *my* wants.[256] I wouldn't have had room for the real Lord, the Lord of everything that is created.

So I went back to my conversation with Jesus. What did he say about praying to him when I was so worried about my efforts? What did he say would happen if I prayed to him? What help would he provide?

I looked back in my scroll. I expected to see the word success after the phrase 'praying to God,' but my memory is short and now I see why one needs to continually turn to God's Word. Success, especially in the form of riches, was not one of the words he used. He used words like 'wisdom'[257] and 'comfort'[258] and 'peace.'[259] Riches would probably make things easier, but He didn't mention that. Then I remembered reading that Solomon prayed, and he received wealth, riches and honor. But that wasn't what he had prayed for. Solomon prayed for wisdom and knowledge and God gave him those, along with what he *didn't* pray for: wealth, riches and honor.[260]

"Can't we pray for success and riches too?" I asked out loud. Didn't Jesus say that anything we ask for in His name he will do?[261] That is true. I remember him saying that. But first we must truly believe, truly love and believe in God. When we do, He will make himself at home within us.[262]

To have God dwell within us is quite an honor, one that should also make us quite humble. Are we then so proud that we will ask for riches? Riches that enable us to provide for ourselves things that we think God won't or is unable to provide? That is very arrogant, not humble at all. Therefore we don't receive what we pray for because we ask with the wrong motive.[263] Jesus said we would do what he did, even greater things than what he did.[264] Just ask in his name, Jesus said, and he would do it.

But there was an addition to this statement. It related to the purpose of asking for anything in his name so he would do it, the purpose being "so that the Son may bring glory to the Father."[265] Successful endeavors that result in gaining wealth do occur from prayer, but they probably happen to serve God's purposes and his will. All prayers are heard and answered, but praying for riches to glorify oneself is probably not Jesus' intention.

So, am I destined to just fail at whatever I do—farming, tending a vineyard, shepherding—one thing and then the next? Jesus had told me that things won't always go like we want. In this world, we will have trouble,[266] but the world judges us by the amount of our success. Is that the correct method for how *we* are to judge ourselves? Jesus said, "God doesn't see us the way the world does, He looks at our heart."[267]

He then gave me the example of Abraham. He wanted a son so badly, and God gave him one, but then God told him to sacrifice him, to kill him. But God was just testing him to see what was first in Abraham's life: love of God and his will or what Abraham himself desired. Abraham proved that God was first, and then God stopped Abraham from harming his son.

The answer then is not to judge ourselves by our successes or failures. What matters most is that we put God first. We are to walk with God, and at the proper time, when He desires, He will make his plans known to us.[268] We need to learn to wait for His timing and, in all we do, walk with God and trust Him while we're waiting.[269]

We shouldn't place our faith in ourselves, or make success our god. We shouldn't look at the troubles that we see now and think that is our destiny. We're looking in the wrong direction. We must fix our gaze on things that cannot be seen. For the things we see now will soon be gone. We need to realize that the things we cannot see are the things that will last forever.[270]

Jesus assured me that even though I may be anxious and fearful, no purpose is accomplished by worrying. I can be comforted in knowing that he has been through it too, and that he was victorious. His victory was for us.[271]

How could I forget what he endured to get to the victory? Jesus went through torture and a gruesome death on a cross. The victory provided a destination for us, a destination beyond this life. In achieving salvation for us, Jesus conquered sin, death and the devil. This wasn't done just for people who were successful and had acquired plenty of wealth, though they are not excluded because of their wealth, it's just that wealth doesn't matter. If it did matter, when people died their wealth would go with them. However, to their disappointment, their wealth is left behind for others. All their busy rushing around ends in nothing. They are unable to even know who will get their wealth and spend it.[272] Then, to perpetuate this vain desire for wealth, people will foolishly fight over this 'left-behind wealth,' forgetting that they are fighting over something that only has temporary value. When they die, they will have to abandon their wealth, and their possessions as well. So if you have wealth, use it to bring honor to God.

So what am I supposed to do? How do I know what God's will is for me? How did I get to where I am, and even more importantly, am I at the place God wants me to be? I pray for wisdom and strength to do what God desires for me.[273] But how do I know what that will be? What should I do? Should I just wait? Waiting isn't as easy as you might think. King David asked God for guidance too, to lead him down the right path, and the answer was to wait patiently for the Lord, be brave and courageous, yes, and wait patiently for the Lord.[274]

David could be confident and boast about not being afraid of anything, but in his heart he felt abandoned, even by his family. I too, sometimes feel alone, not abandoned by a kingdom as David had felt, but on a smaller scale, just looking for a purpose.

I then recalled Jesus saying that I should have been asking him for help. "Come and talk with me," he'd said. In my heart, I responded, "Lord, I am coming.[275] I want to know your will!" David himself received this message. So then I shall pray too. I'll pray not only for wisdom but peace as well.

When one is waiting on God, it's easy to get distracted. You try to put your faith in God, but you see wicked people succeed in their ways. It is hard to remain still and wait patiently.[276] But I continue to pray, and I do so constantly. I must admit I am happier seeking God and not following the ways of treacherous people. I remain confident that by following God's ways, my family and I will be blessed and prosperous[277]—prosperous by God's standards.

Jesus instructed me not to follow the ways of evil people, or the ways of the world which slyly corrupts, making things shadowy. God's desire is not for man to travel the worldly path. It's like trying to walk in the dark: we usually end up tripping over something. He said to follow His ways; He'll light the path so we'll get to the right destination.[278] By following him, we won't copy the behavior and customs of this world. We'll change and be transformed into new people. Then we'll learn what God's plans are for each of us: His will, which is perfect.[279]

So, here I am, sitting and writing, with my son nearby, watching the sheep in the pasture, fulfilling "plans" that the creator of the universe *had* for me. Why would He be concerned about me? How could I fit into any of His plans? How did I end up here at this particular point in time?

Had I arrived a few weeks earlier, Jesus would have been on his way to Jerusalem. In fact, I left later than normal this season because my wife was ill. I took care of her for a while, but it wasn't until Meira's sister had returned from Jerusalem that I was able to get provisions ready for Daniel and me in addition to all the things Meira would need while I was gone. Just when I was ready to leave, our mule wandered away, causing me to stay one more day searching for it. (I thought that was odd because I was sure that I had secured the pen door.)

I am beginning to understand that the task he "had" for me, to write, was much more involved than just the act of writing. Maybe these weren't random events or coincidences. Maybe I'm just unable to comprehend all the ways of God. Not only was the timing of my departure adjusted, but so too the route for my grazing tour, mainly by the strange, rainless storm that redirected the sheep, Daniel and me to this wonderful place.

But why was *I* chosen for this? God only knows. To think that so many incidents were involved in having me here is beyond comprehension. I am only aware of a few of the events of these past few weeks. How many more were under God's directions to bring about the results that He desired? How can God do this when there are so many people?

I tried to imagine the magnitude of intertwining so many lives, each touching another in countless relationships and contacts. I glanced out at the field and considered the nearly 100 sheep I'm in charge of. I'm concerned about each one of them. They might look the same to a stranger, but I can recognize each one.

The sheep also have their own ways. I've been able to distinguish them from each other since they were born. How much more God is able to know than I am, being merely a man! He is responsible for the creation of every person;[280] of course He is able to recognize each one of us and guide each of our paths.[281]

Is my whole life then a series of events that take me from one place to another, interacting with strangers and friends alike, to serve God's purposes?[282] Failures and successes alike, all working to...working to what? I wasn't sure.

Once more I looked back at the different things I had done in my life. I tried to remember significant times that might have had an impact on me, or different people who may have influenced me, even thinking back to when I lived in my father's house. There are events that I can remember and some people who were kind and knowledgeable, but nothing stands out. Yes, there have been highlights such as marriages and births, but mainly my life has been about perseverance. But I have also persevered with my belief in God, and perhaps this was the most important thing of all. Jesus had referred to people like me as noble and with a good heart, those who hear his word, believe it and persevere, thus encouraging others to do the same.[283] This undoubtedly was the key.

All the previous steps in life, inconsequential to me, were indeed significant and were building upon each other to bring me to this place, both physically and in my soul. And it doesn't stop with today. I must continue on with confidence and hope, for the same God who was with me yesterday will be with me tomorrow, too.

As for why the events of my life have happened as they have, perhaps I should develop the attitude Mordecai displayed when he gave advice to his niece Esther during a crucial time and relate it to myself: "Who knows but that I have been put in this place for such a time as this?"[284]

Writing for Jesus is quite an honor now, providing unbelievable satisfaction. But a few weeks ago my confidence in myself, regarding how successful my life had been, was quite different; at least that is the way I judged it. Had I known what lay ahead, I would have felt much differently. If I had known, or realized, that my life was in God's hands all along, I would have, and should have, walked with contentment and joy. I didn't realize that I wasn't working alone, I wasn't traveling alone, and I wasn't contemplating alone.

I must therefore take a humble approach when analyzing the journey of my life so far and my life in the days to come, wherever or whatever that may be. I understand now and accept that some people will receive wealth or possessions that may make them happy, but true contentment will come with a trusting faith in God.

Now I'm beginning to understand the peace that Jesus talked about. The peace is only available from him, not from anything the world has to offer. Peace is the restoring of our relationship with God that Jesus accomplished on the cross: the gift of salvation. It is free; we just have to accept him as our Savior.

The peace Jesus offers will provide incomparable riches, yet this treasure won't be fully received until we enter eternity. This might be a simplistic way of looking at it, but it is true: all that any of us has, no matter how precious, will remain here when we die. We will take with us what we began with at our birth: nothing.[285]

All in all, I still come back to the basic and trustworthy saying; "Trust in the Lord with all your heart; do not depend on your own understanding. Seek His will in all you do, and He will show you which path to take."[286]

I was just about to set my pen down and put the lid on the jar of ink when I looked up and saw Jesus standing in the shade of a tree not very far away. He was smiling and nodding his head in agreement. Even though he was by the tree, he had been listening to my thoughts all along. We had just had another conversation, but this one had been done in the Spirit.

He called out "Peace be with you," turned, and headed back up the ridge, in the direction of the stairway.

Day 27 – Worship

Daniel and I often climb up the ridge to see Jesus at night; we never cease to marvel at or tire of this magnificent sight. Ever since my mishap that first night, when I saw Jesus and the Golden Stairway, I've been very cautious on the ridge. But now that we've climbed up there many times, it has become familiar ground. We know where to step and how to avoid the hole that swallowed my foot and leg.

The path on the ridge leads to an ideal location for viewing Jesus and the stairway. We don't peek around the corner as I first did, but we do realize this is a rare privilege we've been granted, and we always approach with upmost respect. Even though the stairway is very close and easily visible, it's not accessible. The ledge we stand on drops down suddenly, and it is not at all safe to climb down. In fact, the stairway is separated from all the cliffs around it. There are other ledges similar to what we view from, but none have access to the stairway, as far as we can deduce. The stairway must be supported by a platform that rests on an adjacent ridge (I'm making a guess now as I am unclear to its structure). Large rocks provide a comfortable place for us to sit.

Yesterday, we herded the sheep together for the night and then completed our tasks by the time the sun was about to set. We climbed up the rocks, bringing along our cloaks (for the nighttime breeze is cooler up on the ridge), and our staffs to assist our climb. After the initial climb, we proceeded up the path. There was a tall wall of rock on our left and our camp down below on our right. The path eventually turned to the left through a pass in the wall, a narrow corridor with a wall of rock on both sides.

As we approached this final turn of the path, our hearts begin to race with anticipation because the rocks were lit by the glow from the Golden Stairway. We felt fearful because it was such an unearthly sight, though welcoming as well. The pathway continued a short distance and then the wall of rock ended, and the path opened onto a ledge about the size of two small huts. But at this point we usually stop in wonderment because directly in front of it is the Golden Stairway. We have yet to become accustomed to the magnificence of this heavenly sight, which still causes us to stagger over to sit on rocks which long ago had dislodged and fallen from above.

The angels, who also cast a glow into the darkening evening, were busy at their tasks and ascending and descending the stairway. Each angel appeared to have an assignment; some were making preparations that I couldn't comprehend, others stood guard.[287] Jesus wasn't there yet and we hadn't seen him at our camp that day, either.

The stairway rises into the sky; the top is not visible as it disappears into the heavens. Just in front of us, the stairway widened and divided as it approached the base, creating a portion on each side of the throne on which Jesus would soon sit. More angels stand guard around the throne.

Suddenly, everything began to get brighter: the stairway, the throne, the angels and the walls of the rocks around us. It was then that we realized that Jesus was approaching. He too was dazzling white, but brighter than everything around him.[288] As he walked to the throne, I realized he was walking on what looked like a sea of glass or sparkling crystal.[289] It surrounded the throne, but it wasn't there before he arrived. I would have noticed it.

I had heard that Jesus could walk on water, but thought it was just a story made up by some fishermen.[290] Now I was seeing something equally unbelievable. He must also walk on this crystal sea when he visits our camp. I recalled how Philip said he just appeared in the locked room with the disciples.[291] Jesus has so much power we can't comprehend.

As Jesus neared the throne, all the angels stopped what they were doing, bowed and worshipped him. We did the same.

After a while, our eyes adjusted to the brilliance, and then we realized that others were watching from the surrounding rocks, but they were unlike Daniel and me. All around us and stretching into the sky were angels, heavenly sentries. Some stood on small ledges; others appeared to be floating near the steep walls. Though stationed like guards, they did not seem concerned that evil would appear, since even those spirits must obey Jesus. These sentries were worshipping as well.

Oh, what joy in this brilliant sight, this heavenly sight! Jesus said he is the light of the world. People are in darkness, a spiritual darkness, and he shines the light, leading them to the one true God.[292] Once you see this light, *see Jesus*, it's difficult to keep it to yourself. How can this light—this joy—be concealed?[293] In fact, Jesus does want us to tell everyone.[294] How will they know if we don't tell them?[295]

We could feel the warmth from the light radiated by Jesus, and experience had taught us that we would carry this radiance with us when we left.[296]

Daniel stared in awe. He, too, recognized that we were witnesses to something very unique. I leaned over and whispered, "Makes you want to start singing for joy."

A big smile from Daniel let me know he agreed. If everyone could see this, they would never worship another. Their praises would never be half-hearted or misguided.

Worshiping God will be different now. Since the crucifixion on the cross, we can go to God ourselves: it is not restricted.[297] Jesus has washed away our impurities so that we can approach God and receive His grace.

Jesus deserves such enormous praise. Daniel and I make a very small choir; what joy it would be to have a large group singing and praying and worshipping our God. Jesus said if two or more are gathered for his sake, he will be there,[298] but he is always with us if we allow him to enter our hearts. I think he's just encouraging us to worship together. God wants us to always worship him.

Now, we don't have to worship only at the temple. We are able to go to God at all times, in all places. Jesus said we'll be able to worship in spirit and truth.[299] His spirit is everywhere. We can praise him at all times, and never stop. But we shouldn't just worship alone; we need to worship with others and spread God's love.[300] As for truth, we must follow what God has said, not what man decides for man's purposes.

We watched Jesus and the angels for quite a while but now the hour was getting late and I could see that Daniel was getting weary. He was too big for me to carry down the cliff, so I motioned that it was time to leave.

We bowed down and retreated backwards out of natural respect until we were within the corridor. We turned around and I steadied Daniel. Looking at the Lord's glory for so long required us to pause until our eyes adjusted to the darkness ahead. Eventually we could see the path again. Our glow, our radiance, now lit the path ahead for us and we descended to our camp.

We were quiet as we prepared our beds, contemplating what we had seen and savoring the feeling of being filled with such a satisfying peace. Daniel broke the silence as he lay down. He asked in his broken speech, "Someday will everyone see that?"

"Yes," I said. "He has promised that there will be a time when we shall all live together, God with us." What a wonderful time that will be.[301]

Day 29 – Death

My morning was occupied by writing in this scroll. Since this is a slow process for me, I'm usually a few days behind in recording our conversations. I now took some time to further absorb what we had witnessed two nights ago when Daniel and I climbed up on the ridge.

I watched the sheep graze in the field set aglow by the afternoon sun. When these animals are content, they are slow-moving creatures, so my mind began to wander. I contemplated how fortunate we are to be in this place: being with Jesus, the God of all creation, surrounded by angels, the weather is comfortable, plenty of fine pasture for the sheep and no predators to harm them, Daniel and I are both content, and missing ewes are still returning. I was happy because everything was as one would like it to be; God was nearby and all was well. But God has always been nearby, since the beginning, and everything is not "always well."

Everything was not as it should be everywhere. My thoughts then returned to my home. My wife was ill when I left. I have prayed that good health would be restored to her, and I believe that it will be. Then my mind began to consider my neighbors and members of my family, relatives and friends whom I have loved dearly. I contemplated the suffering they have endured, and my heart became greatly saddened.

Why did the baby, just brought forth and with such joy to his parents, cease breathing after one day and die? Why did the young son of our friends—on the verge of manhood—become ill and need extensive care for many years, at times giving everyone hope that he would conquer the illness, only to succumb to the disease and die, their only son?

Or my mother's sister, dearly loved by all (especially by her husband), who after providing devoted service for many years, showing generosity and care to others when they were ill (especially at the end of their lives), who expressed the love that a strong faith produced during her lifetime, who was an example to all of God's love, was then unfortunate to suffer a lengthy illness herself, wearing her down physically, as well as those close to her, until she too died.

Other incidents come to mind. My wife's good friend since childhood, was just a young woman when she was brutally killed by an evil man for his own desires. And the family across the valley, when the wife who was with child suddenly died—mother and baby both gone. There are more, but the sad memories make me stop.

Why are these people chosen to suffer? Nor do they suffer alone; the ones close to them, the ones who love them dearly, they witness this suffering. When death comes, they endure more: the distress of their loss weighs heavily on their hearts, causing them to be downcast.

I tried to decide if I should ask Jesus about this. Should I question the ways of God or just accept them? Is there an answer to these questions, these confusing thoughts about events which bring such inner grieving deep within one's heart, often to the point of breaking? These events cause many people to question if there is a God. I know that God exists: I have seen him. The answer to why people suffer is not as obvious.

From behind me came the words I had become very familiar with: "Peace be with you." Before I could respond, Jesus told me that there is nothing wrong with asking God questions. David did it quite often and he is still very well thought of.

"Why do people die?" I asked. "Why do children die before they have lived a life? Why do people who have lived good long lives have to suffer at the end? Why do people die suddenly—sometimes violently—randomly?"

Jesus paused for a moment, not so much to gather his thoughts but for mine to slow down so I could be ready to listen and comprehend what he was about to say.

But while my mind was still racing, I blurted out that I knew that death was our punishment for Adam and Eve disobeying God in the garden; because they ate from the tree of the knowledge of good and evil,[302] we would all die and return to the ground as dust, like the dust we were created from.[303]

Jesus said that was true. "Until I return, all men will die."[304]

I told him that we have a difficult time with death. It seems so final to us. After all the struggles and battles, much hardship, toiling to survive—in the end, no matter how fortunate or unfortunate our lives have been, we still finally lose and die.

Jesus reminded me that he does understand the fear of suffering and death. Before he went to the cross, he prayed earnestly about what God had planned for him, the awful suffering and death he would have to endure. In fact, he prayed that he would not have to suffer. At that moment, he was feeling man's emotions and fears, but he also knew that what God had planned was best for him and for all people, and he would be obedient to God's will. He explained that in this time of great distress, he prayed very passionately and God provided comfort to him[305] as he will do for us.

Again he paused. I was ready to listen. Jesus explained that this is why he came. He came to be a light in the darkness of people's lives, a darkness which has always surrounded people's lives from the beginning. It is the dark shadow cast by death. Be assured, he said, that a light has dawned. John's father (John was the one who went before him announcing his arrival) had been given a vision of this purpose.[306] In fact, he was repeating what had been told to Isaiah many years ago: on those living in the land of the shadow of death, a light has dawned.[307]

The end of a person's life—death, has always been in a person's thoughts. Its inevitability has confused him about his purpose in living:[308] what should he do with his life before he dies? Because man fears death, it is also a deterrent from unlawful behavior;[309] God has many commands to which if broken, the appropriate response is death.[310] Man threatens death upon his enemy because it is the ultimate punishment,[311] but his enemy also threatens him. He fears it when danger or illness surrounds him[312] because he knows it won't always be avoided. These are just a few ways darkness surrounds people's lives.

"Remember, Shemaiah, how David talked about 'walking through the valley of the shadow of death'?" Jesus asked.[313] "It wasn't just a nice poetic psalm. He was referring to a real journey on a real path. The valley is between the mountains and the goal is the top of the mountain. Everyone will take this path in the valley. But we don't have to travel this path alone."

Jesus explained that his purpose is to guide us on this path, through this dark valley of death, and lead us to our Heavenly Father and peace.[314] Then he emphasized, "You must not let yourselves be distressed; you must hold on to your faith in God and to your faith in me"[315] and you will cross over from death to life.[316]

He again reminded me of what I had often quickly read over from the ancient writings, mentioning David again and how he understood that his life was just a journey down a path that would lead to eternal life.[317] He referred to himself as a traveler passing through,[318] a stranger here on earth. A traveler realizes that his stay is just temporary. He doesn't hold on tightly to where he has stopped, for he will soon be leaving and eventually he will be at home.

People become confused when Jesus says, "Don't love your life in this world." But the person who loves his life in this world and doesn't look to a life in God's kingdom will not enter it. It's those who believe in Jesus, that he is God's only Son, who care nothing for their life in this world. "They will keep their life for eternity,[319] Jesus said. "There will be a reward for them, and it will be in Heaven."[320]

He further explained that our goal here is not to avoid death. It is to avoid *eternal* death. Jesus often taught the disciples to "not be afraid of those who kill the body but are powerless to kill the soul. Rather, fear only God who has the power to destroy both soul and body in the fires of destruction in hell."[321]

We are not unfortunate to die here. Our fortune or goal is to receive eternal life. We shouldn't misunderstand and think that we can achieve eternal life on our own. Only through God is this possible;[322] only though faith in his Son.[323]

I became confused when Jesus mentioned souls and bodies. I had seen many people put into the grave and they stayed there. Their bodies went back to the soil in the ground as it is written in the holy writings: 'for dust you are and to dust you will return.'[324]

"So what is this 'soul' that you mention?" I asked Jesus.

Jesus then instructed me that man was created in God's image.[325] "Man is both body and soul or spirit. You can see my body; you can see your body. You know that it is something that actually exists, but you also have a soul or a spirit." He explained that "God is spirit,[326] I have a spirit," and then Jesus pointed to me and said, "You also have a spirit. Remember that God gave great wisdom to Solomon, who wrote about what happens when people die: "For then the dust will return to the earth, and the spirit will return to God who gave it."[327]

Jesus related that during his ministry, he encountered many who had lost someone much-loved from their family to death, and sometimes he called back their spirit and their body returned to life. He did that for a young girl just recently.[328]

Then Jesus told about his own death. His body was put in a grave, but before he died he gave his spirit back to God. He proclaimed it so that people would notice and remember that he was spirit *and* body,[329] but sometimes even when something is presented openly before people, they don't comprehend, and though they hear, they don't understand.[330] His body was put in the grave and his soul was in his Father's hands.

Jesus then told me about the power that he had been given: the power God has that has also been given to his Son. He stated that no one can take his life from him. He sacrificed it voluntarily and he has the power to retake it."[331]

Jesus' body did not stay in the grave very long, but long enough for there to be no doubt that he was dead; a large stone was rolled across and secured in the tomb's doorway to ensure that he stayed there.[332] With God's power, he was raised from the dead. His body did not decay (God would not allow that.) David had written that long ago.[333]

A resurrected body and spirit was needed to convince people to believe that he was the Son of God, and to convince his disciples and the many women who provided for them that what he said would indeed occur: that on the third day, he would rise from the dead. This victory over death is promised to all who believe; it is the promise of eternal life.

I listen in wonderment every time Jesus talks about being raised from the dead. His magnificent resurrection! It gives me such joy. It brings such peace and contentment. But then questions enter my thoughts again. Why doesn't the body go to the Father as well? Will our bodies be raised on the third day also? Will our bodies decay? Death creates so many questions.

"Your spirit will be received first," Jesus told me. "This is for all who believe. Remember, God is spirit and man is made in God's image. Even the fellow on the adjacent cross at last believed and his spirit joined me when he died,[334] but his body was buried. Also, the body of the one who didn't believe was buried."

Jesus then reminded me that the body will decay: it will return to the dust of the ground where it came from.

"What about the soul of the one on the cross who didn't believe?' I asked.

"You are right to ask about his soul," Jesus said. "It did not go to a place that could be called a paradise. Where that spirit went it will receive much anguish. This is the place where the angels who sinned were sent to await the final judgment.[335] A great chasm will separate those who believe from the unbelievers while they wait for me to come back."[336]

"Come back?" I asked.

"Yes." Jesus then explained that he will come back to judge the world. Those who have already passed through death and believed in God's Son will have already been enjoying God's blessings and will have nothing to fear with the Judgment Day.[337] Those who are alive when he returns, if they believe, they too will join their brothers in paradise. Those who don't believe and those whose souls have been held in punishment will fear this judgment.[338]

"Don't be surprised!" Jesus said. "All the dead in their graves will hear the voice of God's Son, and they will rise again.[339] Remember that Isaiah wrote: 'Your dead shall live; their bodies shall rise. You who dwell in the dust, awake and sing for joy!'[340] A person's soul will once again be joined to their body."

I wondered what our bodies will be like when Jesus returns for the final judgment. So I hesitantly asked, "Will we have the same broken, worn-out bodies?"

Jesus smiled and patiently explained that the bodies that are resurrected are like seeds planted in the ground. It will be the same way with the resurrection of the dead. Our earthly bodies are planted in the ground when we die, but what will be raised will live forever. Those broken, weak, earthly bodies will be raised in glory and strength: they will be spiritual bodies.[341]

I could now accept and actually realize that death is not some ending point of a lifetime. Earthly struggles and suffering may be over, but a new stage of life commences: a new beginning, so to speak.

For one who believes in God's son, it should almost be a quandary whether your desire is to be here on earth in the body or at home in Heaven with the Lord.[342]

Jesus heard my thoughts and quickly corrected them. "Yes, your desire for Heaven is right, but God has not only determined the places where man should live, and his purpose, He has also determined the times for man's existence.[343] He will guide you along the best pathway for your life and advise you and watch over you.[344] But you can be with the Lord now: worship the Father in spirit."[345]

To ensure that I would make an accurate record, I restated to Jesus what he had been teaching me. I began by saying, "We are not just bodies that go to the grave when we die. We were created with a spirit and when we die, if we believe that you are the Son of God, our spirit will go to be with God. If we don't believe, then our spirit goes to a different place and endures punishment with other unbelievers and enemies of God. You will leave here for a while, and when you return, our bodies will rise from the grave and join our spirits to face the final judgment. This part sounds terrifying."

Jesus then consoled me, assuring me that there is no need to fear or worry.

He told me to remember the words he said: "The person who hears what I have to say and believes in the one who sent me has eternal life—his name is in the Book of Life. He does not have to face judgment; he has already passed from death into life; you know I would only tell you the truth."[346]

I continued my summary by saying, "At the judgment, those who believe will gain a beautiful eternity in Heaven with God, and those who failed to believe will be judged and receive eternal death."

Then I added, "Eternal death can be hard to accept from a God who cares so much about his people and sent his Son to die and redeem us."

But Jesus assured me, "God doesn't want anyone to be lost. He is very patient, wishing all to repent. [347] Everyone has a choice. There are many paths that people can take in their lives, paths that are wide and tempting to travel but they don't lead to life. However, there is only one way to eternal life, and the path to that gate is narrow," he said, "and the road is difficult, and only a few ever find it."[348]

"When will this happen? How much time do people have to make their decision, change their ways and believe?" I asked.

Jesus couldn't answer this question. "No one knows when these things will happen, no one in Heaven, not even I. Only the Father knows."[349]

"Why would people not believe while they have a chance?" I asked him. "If they decide to wait to believe until they saw it happening, it could be too late," I said. "They would have to always be alert in fear that while they were sleeping they would miss their chance."

Jesus agreed, and then said, "There is one thing I do know about my return: it will be when I am least expected."[350]

Again, the thoughts of dying and death and missing loved ones filled my mind, and I began to feel uneasy.

"We still have to get through death and grief when someone we love dies," I said. My heart sank again and my head slumped as I looked downward.

Jesus agreed. "Death is on the path to eternal life but I have conquered it."[351]

He lifted my chin, looked straight into my eyes and said "Don't let yourself be distraught; keep holding on to your faith in God, and have faith in me also."[352]

Then he reminded me that he has overcome the world.

"The sting of death is gone," he said. "I have done what the prophets said, what God has promised. I have ransomed you from the power of the grave; I have redeemed you from death.[353] That is why the disciples will preach so boldly. They will not fear death. They have seen that death has no power."

I tried to comprehend the purpose of the pain suffered when losing one you care so much about.

"I can understand that a long, suffering death is not without some blessing. A person is able to say good-bye to the one dying, and the person leaving this world has a chance to console those who will remain for a while longer. Preparation for the loss can occur, difficult as it may be. But some die suddenly with no warning. Why is this?" I asked.

"Here on earth there are many trials and sorrows,"[354] Jesus said. He, too, understood about grieving, and he brought up when John the Baptist was beheaded. After the disciples told him, he took his grief to his Father, by himself in prayer.[355]

Jesus then gave me some instructions on grief. He impressed on me that God is a merciful Father and a God of all comfort.[356]

"Turn to him and talk to him," Jesus said. "Pray and ask questions. Be assured that the Lord cares deeply when his loved ones die. They are precious in His sight."[357]

Jesus also said that God comforts people in their times of trouble, and we should share this compassion with others when they need to be comforted.[358] People feel alone during times of suffering, grief and loss; knowing that others have been through a similar experience provides great comfort. It helps ease the burden of sorrow that they are carrying. That's why we should stand alongside others and let God's love overflow through us.

When being comforted, we must remember that the separation is not permanent, only an interruption, and that a great reunion will occur. When we provide comfort, we should take the opportunity to teach and remind our grieving friends of this as well.

Our bodies will grow old and die, but our spirit is eternal. Jesus told me that God has put the desire for eternity with Him in the hearts of people, but even so, we are not able to see and understand the ways of God.[359] But one thing is sad: for unbelievers, facing death with no hope is very difficult. How can one comfort another if there is no hope?

Those who believe do not need to fear—paradise awaits us. We can't picture what is on the other side of death. The prophet teased us when he said: "For since the world began, no ear has heard, and no eye has seen a God like you, who works for those who wait for him."[360] If it wasn't for God's spirit, we couldn't begin to imagine what God has prepared for those who love him.[361]

Jesus continued by saying, "Because you have seen that there is life after death—don't lose hope, you are not to grieve like people who don't believe in God's Son—those with no hope. To overcome your grief you must accept comfort, but you must also accept God's will in the events of your life. You are to say, no matter how difficult it may be, "yet not my will, but yours be done." [362]

This acceptance is only possible because of the hope of eternal life which has been bought for us by Jesus. It was bought and paid for on the cross and proven by his resurrection from the dead.

Jesus then gave another reason to look beyond our life here: that Heaven is where he is going and he'll be leaving soon. His presence here after being resurrected from the tomb is just temporary. He has a job to do: preparing a place for us.[363] He says it has many rooms.

It had been a long day of instruction but I was finally seeing how life worked. Death is a stage of life. Separation is hard—very hard—and even though it's only temporary, the tearing apart requires time for healing. This is accomplished by comforting from God and friends. We shouldn't fear death for our loved ones or for ourselves. Death has no permanent hold on us. Across the divide is paradise—also known as Heaven—and life with Jesus. That is where I want to go, where I want *everyone* to go. We won't really be home until then.

Day 3 2 – Heaven

The last few days I have been busy at my flat rock table recording on the scroll our previous conversation regarding the end of earthly life, more commonly known as death. It's hard to overcome ideas that have been with you your entire life, especially when you've seen so many loved ones go to the grave. When thinking logically about death, my fears begin to recede and I can become comfortable with the fact that death is not permanent, that a better place is in our future. This causes me to start wondering what Heaven will be like.

A while ago, Jesus gave me some insight by saying that I wouldn't be disappointed. David wrote in one of his psalms that when God creates, splendor and honor and majesty are before him.[364] Heaven will be magnificent beyond imagination. In fact, God's city—the city where he will live,[365] the New Jerusalem—will be made of precious stones, its gates each made from a solid pearl.[366]

He then repeated a previous statement: "I will be leaving soon to get things ready and to go prepare a place for everyone who believes."[367]

I questioned what he meant when he said 'to go prepare.'

"Isn't Heaven ready for us yet? Isn't it complete? Didn't you tell me that after we die, our spirits go to be with you? God created everything in seven days. Wasn't Heaven finished? Didn't Moses write in the Scriptures that God created the heavens and the earth[368] and He said it was good?"

Jesus then said, "There is a place for your spirit but before you receive your new spiritual body,[369] some things need to be accomplished first. For before the resurrection of the dead, I will create a New Heaven and a New Earth."[370]

I couldn't comprehend what he was telling me. I thought I had misheard what he said. "Did you say 'New Heaven and New Earth'?"

"That is true," Jesus confirmed.

"I realized we had lots of problems on earth, but I always believed that Heaven was in a state of perfection. Isn't Heaven perfect?"

He instructed me: "Recall that sin entered man in the Garden and he was deceived by the serpent; that temptation was the work of Satan and the angels in Heaven that he had also deceived."

I considered for a moment what he was telling me. Then I asked, "Didn't God throw Satan out of Heaven? Or does Satan still have a presence in Heaven?"

To my surprise, Jesus said, "There are still spiritual forces of evil in Heaven."[371]

"When you make a New Heaven what will you do? Will Heaven be cleansed and made perfect?"

"Satan, and all evil forces alongside him, will be cast out of the heavenly realms. This will happen with a great war; it will culminate when Satan battles against the archangel Michael and God's legions of angels. But this final conflict will be short. Michael will be victorious and the devil will be cast out."[372]

"Heaven, like it is, will not remain." Jesus said he had told this to the twelve disciples, but they weren't ready to comprehend. He told me plainly what he had said to them: "Heaven and earth will disappear, but my words will never disappear.[373] This was nothing new that I said. Isaiah mentioned this long ago. You can read it in the scrolls."[374]

Then Jesus mentioned something that won't disappear. It's a special book called the Lamb's Book of Life. The book contains a list of names, the names of those who will remain in Heaven.

"Remember," Jesus said, "that a new agreement, a new contract, has been made, a reconciliation of man—a payment for mankind's sins to God by my death on the cross. God is fulfilling a promise that he made long ago when He said, "I will forgive their wickedness and will remember their sins no more."[375] But in the New Heaven, those who do not believe, the sinful, those whose names are not in the book of life, they will not be allowed in Heaven.[376] Their place will be in the fiery lake of burning sulfur."[377]

Wars and fiery lakes were not my idea of Heaven; I thought it would be a peaceful place. But then Jesus pointed out that that will be the end of the first Heaven.[378] When the judgment comes, Heaven will be the better place to be.[379]

"The New Heaven will be different," he said. "God's home will be among his people! He will live with them, and they will be His people."

He made sure I heard what he said.

"God Himself will be with them. He will wipe every tear from their eyes, and there will be no more death or sorrow or crying or pain. All those things will be gone forever.[380] People may have suffered on earth, but as far as eternity is concerned it will only be for a little while. While they are suffering now, they should be filled with confidence that in Heaven, God will restore them, support them, and strengthen them, and they will live in an unshakable place where you will feel very secure.[381]

Jesus added that above everything else, our main focus regarding Heaven should be the joy of being with God.

"Many years ago, someone like you, a shepherd, understood this quite well," Jesus said. "David, led by the spirit in his psalms, wrote about his longing for living in Heaven. He talked about the joy of being in God's presence and the pleasures of living with him forever,[382] living in the house of the Lord forever,[383] and he poetically wrote about living safely beneath the shelter of his wings."[384]

"When you pass through death to Heaven, you will also have the joy of worshipping God with other believers.[385] Many of those worshipping with you will be those you knew and loved on earth, those who died before you, those who crossed over before you.[386] A grand reunion this will be: a rich welcome into God's eternal kingdom and worship with so many others,[387] including thousands of angels,[388] all joining together to say praises to God their Father. [389] It will be quite an event."

"What about those who died a long time ago, before your resurrection; people such as the old prophets? Will they have a place in Heaven?" I asked.

"Be assured that at the proper time they will receive their reward in Heaven, too,"[390] Jesus answered with emphasis. "What they did was very important and their work will not be forgotten. The words which they wrote long ago are meant to teach people today, and will continue to teach in future days. When you read in the Scriptures of the endurance of those men and of all the help that God gave them in those days, you can be encouraged to go on hoping in your own time.[391] Their tasks were very difficult, and even though many of them suffered for what they did and the words they spoke and wrote, they accomplished what God desired."[392]

"In fact," Jesus added, "there will be rewards for all. When it is time to judge, servants of the Lord, and prophets, and people who are holy, and all who hold His name in reverence, no matter what their status, will receive a reward, each according to what he has done."[393]

It seemed that the more I learned, the more questions I had.

"What will we do in Heaven? Will we work? Will it be hard work?"

"God has always valued work—having a purpose—and God is also always at work.[394] Moses wrote that when God first created man and woman, he put them in a beautiful garden. Their task was to tend and watch over it,[395] to work it and keep it beautiful and receive nourishment from it.[396] This was before everything changed when sin entered them."

It was now late in the day. The sun was just casting its last light to the sky, and stars were beginning to make their appearance. Jesus looked up at the sky and smiled, then complimented God on the magnificence and magnitude of his creation.

Jesus then said, "There will be many different tasks; some people will even be honored to serve God himself in the New Jerusalem.[397] Everyone will serve in Heaven, but just as there are many ways on earth to serve, so will there be different ways in Heaven."

Then, as he looked at the sky and seemed to be studying the stars, he said that there are many heavenly places...[398] and he made a slight gesture to the sky, but he didn't finish the sentence, at least not out loud for me to hear. I wondered how far away these places could be that would require service.

Again, I was reminded that he knows my thoughts.

"Don't worry, especially about hard work.[399] I have always preached that your burden would be light,"[400] he said.

He then explained that usually when he referred to burdens, he meant the rules that so-called religious leaders often forced people to follow to win so-called "favor" from God, usually for their own ambition or greed. But God takes care of his people.

As for heavenly service, Jesus said, "You wouldn't expect that I would bring you to Heaven for hard labor? What role or service each person will be rewarded with is something that will be determined later, at the proper time."[401]

Then he gently rebuked me by saying, "First you're concerned that your life ends in death and then you're concerned that you won't like where you're going—even when it's eternity in Heaven. Believe me when I say it will be paradise.

"Paradise is not a place for constant work, either." Jesus added. He recalled that over the past three years, he preached to weary people to come to him and he would give them rest.[402]

"Be assured that there will be rest for the believers, especially for those who will suffer when the end is drawing near, the end of the first earth and first Heaven,[403] unlike those who will continue to follow Satan and will never find rest."[404]

He then further explained the New Jerusalem: he called it "God's city."

"It will be magnificent; what a sight is in store for God's people! The gates, which I mentioned before, are each made of a solid pearl; there will be twelve of them. The main street will be made of pure gold, polished like clear glass.[405] There will also be a crystal clear river flowing from the thrones of God and his Son, down the center of that golden street."[406]

"You've often mentioned 'at the proper time.' When will that be?" I asked.

Jesus then reminded me once again, "Only my Father knows."[407]

Jesus might not know *when*, but I am certain about one thing: I want to be on God's side, as far away from the fiery lake as possible.

Then Jesus once again encouraged me to trust him, saying, "Don't worry, I'll come back—and when I do, I'll take you to be with me.[408] I always do what I promise." [409]

Day   33   –   Privilege

"You don't realize the opportunity you have been given...Many have longed to see what you've seen.[410]...God walking visibly among his people is something rare. That is what Heaven will be like: God among his people.[411] In Heaven, people will have actual contact with God and be able to actually see Him...What I am saying is not just to you. People at this point in time, people in this small area of creation have had a unique privilege...These last few years many people have seen me—there have been thousands.[412] Many also saw me die on the cross, because Jerusalem was filled with people for Passover. A smaller group of people, but enough that it can't be denied, have seen me since leaving the grave; at least 500."[413]

These were some of the comments Jesus made today.

He continued by saying, "It didn't use to be like that, man not being able to see God. When man was still in the Garden, God was there, but that all changed.

"During the time of Moses, God talked to him from a bush full of fire,[414] or in a cloud,[415] or out of fire on a mountain."[416]

"There was one time that God did let people see him. Moses, 70 elders and a few others went up on the mountain and saw God (but not his face) and only from a distance. He wasn't standing on the mountain like they were, but on a platform (Moses compared it to clear sapphire). They had a meal with him.[417] After this, God did not allow people to try and see him except for Moses.[418] He made sure they showed the proper respect and learned to fear Him as all powerful."

"There has never been another prophet in Israel like Moses whom the Lord knew face to face.[419] However, God still made contact with people; sometimes through angels, sometimes in dreams, and also through many prophets. God's methods are unlimited. In fact, one time, when Elijah was discouraged and hiding in a cave on a mountain, God spoke to Elijah in a whisper.[420]

"Believe me," and Jesus pointed at me, "a great many prophets and good men have longed to see what you are seeing and they never saw it. Yes, they longed to hear what you are hearing and they never heard it. Even kings desired this."[421]

I was happy to be in such a privileged position, but at the same time I felt unworthy, because I had done nothing to deserve this honor. But then, everything God gives to us is free—especially salvation. That is his method for us.[422]

Jesus then said, "The prophets and others searched,[423] longing to see me and to receive this gift of salvation that was promised. They spoke about this promise, even though they didn't know when or completely understand all that the Spirit of God was telling them. They inquired passionately when this would happen, but they came to accept that the events they were professing would not occur in their lifetime. But you are fortunate; these events have been made plain to you."[424]

"They all died before seeing the promise, but they had faith and looked forward to being with God in Heaven, which He was preparing for them,"[425] he added.

I wondered why Jesus was telling me these things.

He continued, "The people you have read about in the Scriptures all had faith in what they believed; faith that what they heard was true. They delighted in doing what they were commanded to do, but the fear of God was in them."[426]

"The fear of God?" I asked.

"Yes, God is not to be taken lightly or carelessly. Do you remember what happened if someone entered forbidden areas of the temple, especially the Most Holy Place,[427] or if someone touched or even looked into that special acacia chest—the one that contained the stone tablets, the jar of manna, and Aaron's staff[428]—called the Ark of the Lord?"[429]

"I recall being taught what would happen: the result would be death," I answered.

"The consequences of many people who disobeyed or refused to give God the proper respect have been recorded. Do you want me to list them?"

"No—I can understand the fear of God," I said.

"But not completely. You must understand that all that is created was by His hands: everything you can see and everything you *can't* see."[430]

I thought for a moment and remembered how the Scriptures start: "In the beginning God created the heavens and the earth."[431] Mountains and valleys, hills and fields, oceans and rivers. Then of even more magnificence, everything in the sky above: the moon and sun, the stars and beyond them, what I can't even imagine.[432]

"I can understand," I said.

"There is more," Jesus said. "God gave life to all people and to everything that lives."[433]

I considered what Jesus was saying, and then I said: "Everything living in the sea and every living thing in the air,[434] and all that moves on the land,[435] and then He created man and woman."[436]

"Now I understand the fear of God: that He deserves our reverence for the power He has, and our awe for what He has done. There is no other," I said.

Then Jesus made me realize the purpose of our discussion. In order to fully appreciate what has been done, to realize the tremendous love of God that allowed the sacrifice of His son on the cross, we must first grasp the fear of God.

The prophets feared God. Their hope was in the truth that God loved his people, and that His love is unfailing.[437] This faith and hope overflowed into sharing the message with others.

When a person realizes God's place in their life, and that everything belongs to God, including our reverence, honor and fear, then we begin to grow in wisdom.[438]

Jesus then said, "My good friend John most recently displayed this wisdom when he baptized people along the Jordan."

Jesus has mentioned John several times. John's purpose was to prepare people for Jesus' arrival and baptize them.

"What was the purpose of the baptisms?" I asked.

"It showed that people had turned to God to receive forgiveness for their sins."[439]

I looked at Daniel and he nodded, so I asked, "Can we be baptized too?"

Then Jesus led us to the far side of the sheep's grazing field to the small stream where we gathered our water. He bent down and, cupping some water in his hand, poured the water on our heads and said, "I baptize you in the name of the Father and of the Son and of the Holy Spirit."[440]

What joy we had this day! Daniel had a smile on his face until he went to sleep that night, which wasn't until after we climbed the ridge to view the stairway again.

While Daniel lay sleeping, I spent quite a while considering what Jesus had said today. Unable to sleep, I looked into the night sky. God truly is powerful to create all that glimmers far above us, and we can probably see only a small portion. Fear of God, I thought; how can we not have it?

Seeing so many stars also made me realize that so many days have passed before this day. I had to admire all the people in the past that put their faith and hope in God, whom they hadn't seen, yet filled with love, they proclaimed God's messages.[441] I, too, am filled with God's love, and need to share this with others. This is what motivated so many.

Our discussions this day showed that faith and hope are important, but I have seen Jesus and his conquering of the grave, and have witnessed his love. What remains now, I realize, is greater than these—and that is love. [442]

Day 34 – Love

Once again I was instructing Daniel on the ways of a shepherd, but this time I was more patient. We had a good time, too.

We started by going back to the stream where Jesus baptized us; what an honor. It was while we were there that I noticed stones in the stream, worn smooth over the years, which would be ideal for slinging.

I used to be quite accurate with the sling; I'm still not that bad. When I was young, I even won some contests.

During each of the shearing seasons we would have competitions. We all pitched in to get the sheep sheared—we held the sheep while the older men sheared them. When our tasks were completed, the women joined together and washed the wool with lye in the stream. Once it was clean, they beat the water out of the wool and then arranged it to dry on rocks. While the women were busy, the younger boys would show off their skils—one of which was slinging stones at targets.

Daniel and I hung some dried flowers from trees to be used as targets and then I held class on the fine points of slinging. We had done this before, but it will require more lessons before he gets the correct motion; it's a little difficult for Daniel. We had many laughs, and scared a few of the sheep as well. Yes, we had a good time today.

We've had many good days here. I've had tremendous joy and a release from the usual concerns of life while being in this beautiful pasture, sheltered not only by the rocky ridges, but even more so by the protective care of God's Son himself and a legion of his heavenly angels. But I have a deep longing to be with my wife again, whom I have loved since my youth.

Daniel has also been asking about his mother, more so than he normally would on a journey of this type. When we left her she was ill, and her sister was looking after her. I have prayed for her health and have been given a peace and confidence that all will be well with her, but I do miss her terribly and look forward to being with her again. I desire not only to be able to express my love to her but to share this new knowledge and understanding of our creator, our magnificent God and his Son, our redeemer.

I shared these thoughts with Jesus and he explained that these feelings I have are good. Love is a gift from God. When we truly love, we display proof that we are children of God, that we know God.[443] Now if you don't have love for others, then you don't know God; for loving others is one of the ways you prove that God is inside of you.

You can be certain that God has shown His love: his love for his creation, His people and all people. That love is not only for the Jews but also for non-Jews. He showed this love in a magnificent way, too. Jesus explained that God proved His love by sending him to this world, sending His only Son, and that He was to give life to all people through him.[444] There is not a greater demonstration of God's love.

Jesus explained that throughout his ministry, he taught that we are to love our enemies, love those who do the wrong things. As I write this, I realize that is a difficult statement to accept, but then he said that his Father did that to us. While we were still sinners,[445] God sent his Son to pay the price, the penalty, for our evil, disobedient ways—and this was not because we loved God first.[446] No, we are not decent enough to deserve credit for that. He sent his Son because he loved us first. Now we have no excuse. What can we give back that can compare when we have had our sins forgiven? In addition, we are given eternal life as well. What an indescribable gift and expression of love!

I realized that we are so small compared to everything that God has created that we have nothing to give to God to show our thanks: we have empty hands and empty pockets. But Jesus said that there is something we can do. With God's love lavished on us, filling us and living within us, to make this love complete, we should love others as well. When you're filled with love, filled with God's presence, how can you keep it to yourself? How can you not love others?

This love doesn't flow to you as if it comes from a small watering hole that might run dry if you share it. No, it is more like a great waterfall that will never cease, filled by an ocean of love.

"Let your love overflow to others," Jesus said.[447]

"My wife and son; I already love them. Do you mean those others we are related to by blood or marriage? I love most of them. There are a few family members, siblings of my parents, the cantankerous ones that I don't associate with very much, but I am close to some.

I thought for a moment.

"How *do* we show love to others?" I asked. But Jesus seemed to be waiting while I thought more about it.

After a few moments, I said, "There are some neighbors...they have the field to the south of us. We don't seem to have much in common. The others, I believe I have treated them fine. I did hear that the one neighbor was sick."

"Did you take some food to them?" Jesus asked.

"Well...no," I said sheephishly.

"What about that other neighbor?"

"That other neighbor?" I paused for a moment. "Do you mean the one with the unruly son? He went to prison."

"Did you visit him?" Jesus said.

"Well...no. But I am kind to the vendors in the village," I rebutted.

"But there was that one vendor..."

"I think I know who you mean. Well, I can't be at fault if he can't count right."

"Shemaiah." Jesus said disappointedly.

"Yes, it was to my favor. I should have said something."

"That wasn't the only time, either."

"You mean that man that had the hole in his bag?

"Yes."

"...and his money fell out."

"Yes."

"You see everything," I softly admitted. "He probably didn't even miss it," I tried to lie.

"But you found out that he did miss it and you still didn't say anything," Jesus corrected.

"How was I to know that some of it was for the temple and the rest to buy food for his family?" I replied pitifully.

"If that was your money that was lost, wouldn't you want somebody to return it to you?" Jesus asked. "Do what you want others to do. You should do good always. You should show love."

"I did give some money to a little girl who didn't have very nice clothes. I thought it might help."

"That's a start," Jesus said.

"Yes, I had just done well selling some wool, better than I had expected. I guess I could have given a little more. I guess God had blessed me."

"He will bless you more. Your generosity will flow back to you." Jesus said.

"I have noticed that in the past," I said. "We gave some extra tunics to a neighbor that needed them. Then a few days later I was injured and my wife spent considerable time tending to me. Another neighbor brought over some stew, with plenty of meat, already cooked. My wife cried tears of joy at this sign of compassion."

"And there's more," I added. "Another neighbor then helped Daniel bring in the sheep after some wild animal which had been lurking around the field scattered them."

I paused for a moment.

"I guess they were showing love to us—weren't they?"

Jesus nodded. Then he asked,

"Now if your neighbor, a neighbor that you love, has a child, don't you also love the child and you would do anything for that child if your neighbor asked you?"

"Yes, I would," I replied.

"Well, God has children too. God gives to the man or woman, boy or girl, who believes in me the right to become a child of His—a child of God.[448] So how should you treat one of God's children? If you are a child of God, isn't your neighbor like your brother or sister?"

"Yes," I answered timidly.

"So if God loves you and provides for you, doesn't this bring you comfort and joy? You should be thankful for these blessings from God. Shouldn't you also share this joy with others?"

"Now, about your question "How do you show love to others?" Jesus asked.

"I guess I already knew. Maybe it isn't that difficult after all."

Day   3 8   –   S e r v a n t

Our conversation was more difficult today, but not because of the subject. Jesus began by informing us that his time here has almost come to completion. He then reminded me, "Don't forget what you have written down. Apply these things to your life."

Jesus' announcement surprised me, and at first, I couldn't absorb what else he was saying. He had warned us that he would be returning to Heaven to be with his Father, but since a specific day was never mentioned, I assumed we still had plenty of time together.

Daniel also heard Jesus' say that he would be leaving soon, so this day he kept himself very near, as if he wanted to store up as much of Jesus' presence as possible.

Jesus was aware that my thoughts had wandered, but eventually my focus returned and I was able to listen more intently.

He began by sternly saying: "Do you know who I am after these past few weeks? Do you believe that I love you? Do you believe that God is not angry with you; that God loves you[449] and cares for you?[450] Do you understand that what has been done was for a purpose: to bring you close to God?"[451]

The corners of my eyes began to gather tears when he asked me these questions.

"Of course I know who you are," I responded. "I couldn't believe more. You have shown me so much: the scars on your hands and feet, the throne, the stairway, the angels...and the words you have spoken. You are the Son of God. How could I not believe?"

It frightened me that he would question me that way, but then he smiled. Later I came to understand that he asked these questions for my benefit. He was testing me so I would know how *I* would react when the time came that I must give a testimony of my belief in Jesus.[452]

Then, in a gentler tone, he said, "I have given you many things to write about and you have recorded them well. My time *here* is coming to an end and I have a few more words of instruction for you."

"Don't forget what you have written down. Apply the words to your life, but don't use the privilege you've been given as a reason to be proud or arrogant.[453] Follow my example and do as I have done.[454] Be a servant to others."

"What do you mean," I asked, "be a servant?"

"I came as a servant to serve all people, and you should also serve others;"[455] be a humble messenger acting in my behalf.[456] Let people know. Tell them to repent and believe the good news.[457] I'll say it again; don't use your knowledge to build yourself up. Putting yourself above others is not a way of showing love. God takes care of the humble person, and they will receive much.[458] Remember, God's grace was shown to you: forgiving your sins, washing them away. This was not because of anything you did, but because of God having mercy on you.[459]

"But what do I do as a servant?" I asked.

"As a servant, don't let yourself think you are rich now in what you know and what you believe. Remember how spiritually poor you were, how sinful you used to be. Use the knowledge you now have to lead others—especially the ones who realize their spiritual poverty—to the cleansing of their sins and eternal life in God's Kingdom.[460] Tell them what has been done for them. Tell them that God's blessing is there for them. Those who realize this and accept God's grace will be welcomed in Heaven."

"As a servant, also show comfort to those who suffer from loss: loss of loved ones, loss of purpose, loss of hope, and loss of direction because of evil in their life and longing to change.[461] Show them that God cares.

"As a servant, when you find people who don't follow the world's ways and are not full of pride, you can serve them as well. As for those who are filled with pride, tell them about God's grace too. Show them the only way to eternal happiness."

"As a servant, encourage those who do seek and desire to know God. Don't hold back. Tell them all you know. Let them be your friend. They'll help you to see God as well. Follow my example and do as I have been doing, telling you all I know, as you are my friends."[462]

"As a servant, help people in all ways. Show compassion and mercy. Remember that whatever you ask in my name, bringing glory to the Father, will be granted.[463] Don't help others so you can receive praise. Do it quietly, and let your reward come from God."[464]

"As a servant, keep your heart and motives pure. Many lose their way, but hold on to your desire to see God. Worship him and serve him only.[465]

"As a servant, when you serve, seek the peaceful way by showing love. Love can cover up many sins and allow the message of God's grace to be received.[466]

"Lastly," Jesus said, "as a servant you will face persecution. Those who testify about me will be persecuted, so don't be surprised.[467] The evil one will try to dissuade you any way he can; that is why I questioned you so intently before. Your actions when you are tested will encourage others to have faith,[468] but don't worry, God's spirit will instruct you in what to say when that happens.[469]

"Don't let others change you to become like the people of this world. Let God and his Holy Spirit shape your heart, and through the events of your life, you will learn what God desires for you, and that His plans are good and perfect."[470]

Daniel and I will be sad when Jesus returns to Heaven. We'll miss being with him. Once he goes, we won't see the scars in his hands and feet anymore. They are a constant reminder of the suffering he endured for us. They are proof that he is the ultimate servant: he gave his life for us so that we could be with God. I'll gladly serve him and tell everyone the good news.

We should have been expecting his departure announcement; it was God's plan all along. Maybe the day when he returns to judge the world will be as equally unexpected.

Day 39 – Jars

Before going to sleep last night, I made my nightly climb up the ridge to see the Golden Stairway, taking extra caution as usual to avoid the hole into which my foot plunged that first night. As I progressed down the path, I came across two clay jars next to that same hole. They weren't here before. Jesus must have placed them there, or perhaps his angels had done so. If he could create the heavens and the earth and all creation, he could surely create two clay jars. I would have to ask him about them tomorrow.

This morning, I awoke to a voice from above. As my eyes began to focus I realized that Jesus was calling us. He was standing above us on the ridge, waving his arms and motioning us to come up. I quickly woke Daniel up and we climbed up the rocks to where Jesus waited.

We found him standing next to the clay jars. He told me that the jars were for me, for the scrolls.

"Put the scrolls in the linen bags and put one scroll in each jar," he said. "Each jar has a lid to protect the contents." He then bent down and pointed into the hole. "Set the jars on the raised ledge; they will be protected there. Cover the hole with rocks and then spread gravel and dirt into the cracks. That should do well."

At this, I was confused. What purpose would all this work serve if it was just going to be hidden in a hole in the rocks? Many hours had been required to write what was contained on these sheepskins. So I cautiously asked, "Why did I make a record on the scrolls?"

Realizing my disappointment, he put his hand on my shoulder. He then said: "Others will also write. Some will tell details of my many miracles and my teachings, and of the events leading up to the crucifixion and afterwards at the empty tomb. Some writings will require more thought to be understood, and one person will write at length about an extensive vision of the end times and the defeat of Satan's rule over man on earth.

"Remember what I told you about the prophets of long ago? All those words they wrote were meant to teach people. When people read in the Scriptures of the endurance of those men and of all the help that God gave them in their days, others will be encouraged to go on hoping in their own time.[471]

"Your writings on the scroll will also serve a purpose at the proper time."

Jesus then revealed to me: "At different times, God allows tangible evidence to be exposed to help those whose faith is weak and to confound those who are stubborn and defy the living God. Man must be continually reminded with new evidence that the Father does truly exist, but blessed are those who haven't seen but believe.[472] Satan tries to convince people that God doesn't exist, so at different times God allows items to be discovered to help bring those who are lost back home to God."

"What kind of items?"

"Some are very important, very precious, such as the long cloth, the shroud, that covered my body and the separate cloth for my head when I was buried in the tomb. Ancient cities or civilizations will be uncovered that will prove the Scriptures accurate. Man, with Satan's help, will try to disprove the evidence, but the faithful will not be turned aside.

"Other writings will also be discovered, and you are to be a part of that. Go to Jerusalem...," and then he paused. Whenever he talked about Jerusalem, his expression became stern. Then he commented, "Of all people, they should have understood me, but the way to salvation was hidden from them; their enemies will be very destructive and very thorough."[473]

The way he made the statement was almost like a command or a verdict being announced by a judge. "When will this happen?" I asked.

He didn't give me a specific time, but I reasoned that it would be soon.

I was then given new instructions. He reminded me that when we first talked, he said he had plans for me; the writing I have been working on is just one of the tasks. Another task he had planned for me would involve more time and require some travel and even some risk, but Jesus assured me that I would be able to complete this task.

Once again he said, "Go to Jerusalem and then to Arimathea where you will find a man named Joseph, he was in Jerusalem but he has been sent back to Arimathea. He is a member of the Council—a good man.[474] He has been told to welcome you. He has a cup to show you and a special way to remember me. Tell Joseph to remove the ancient scrolls from Jerusalem before it is too late. You should assist him. You will find places to store them safely, out of the way of destruction, near the Dead Sea."

He didn't explain to me how this could be accomplished or how the priests would allow someone to take the scrolls from the temple, but he did say the spirit would instruct me more at the proper time. He then again assured me that I would be able to complete this task. This second assurance brought a chill to me, but it disappeared quickly when I looked at Jesus.

He then turned from discussing Jerusalem and went back to the scrolls I was working on. Jesus convinced me that my writings are also important.

"My words will not return to me empty,"[475] he said. "You are to show that I don't require much;[476] I was dead but now I am alive, and those who believe in me will receive the gift of eternal life."

"Tomorrow," and this was when he said it plainly, "I will go with the eleven to Bethany, the Mount of Olives,[477] and then I will return to be with my Father at His right hand."[478]

"When you have finished writing, put your scrolls in these jars. There will be a time when they will need to be read." Then he went and touched each jar below the lid. When he removed his fingers, I could see the Greek letters Alpha and Omega on the jars.

Alpha and Omega—the first and last letters of the alphabet. The beginning and the end.[479] He was here at the creation and will be here for eternity. Nobody can claim that except God.

Jesus then provided me with great relief when he said, "Go home to your wife. Your prayers were answered; she is well. When you prayed for her, she was healed. She misses you both very much. After you return home, make preparations to leave your sheep in your pasture and go to Jerusalem. Spread the word of salvation everywhere you go."

After these final instructions, it was time to say our farewells. Jesus went over to Daniel and they talked softly for quite a while. At first there were a few laughs, and then I saw Jesus wipe tears from Daniel's eyes. They embraced in a long hug. When they separated, Daniel nodded his head up and down. Even though I couldn't hear him, I could tell that he was saying he would be ok.

Jesus came over and hugged me, too.

"You won't be left alone," Jesus said, "I will send my helper, God's Holy Spirit."[480]

"Now I must go," he said, adding, "I will prepare a place for you and for the rest of the believers as well."[481]

As Jesus turned and walked toward the Golden Stairway, he began to get brighter—a white brilliance. Even though the sun was already bright, he was brighter still. I turned to point this out to Daniel and saw that he had a glow as well. It wasn't nearly as bright as Jesus', but it was definitely apparent. But Daniel didn't see my astonishment, for he was holding out his hands and alternately looking at one and then the other. A big smile spread across his face.

We headed back down the rocks, where the sheep were beginning to stir, and began tending to them. I then looked out at the field: standing in the middle were two more ewes. The flock was nearly back to its original number.

Day 40 – Home

Another beautiful sunny day, but I was saddened when I climbed up the ridge and to my disappointment found that the Golden Stairway was gone. No angels ascending and descending. No platform with the royal chair with Jesus sitting there. Tears filled my eyes. I heard a noise behind me and thought Daniel had followed me up. I turned around and was startled to see one of the heavenly angels standing in front of me.

I started to bow down when he stopped me.

"Don't be sad looking for Jesus," he said. "He is with the eleven now; today Jesus will return to Heaven, just as he said. At the time God has appointed he will come back, just as he also said."[482]

Then the angel disappeared.

I went back down the ridge and told Daniel what I had seen, and then took him up the ridge so he could confirm my news with his own eyes. He had many questions, but he understood almost better than I, and kept repeating to himself, "Trust in Jesus." That must have been part of his private conversation yesterday.

We tended to the sheep. Just as we were getting ready to take them out to the field for grazing, one more ewe walked between some bushes into the field. Our flock was now complete: none had been lost and all appeared healthy. Another prayer had been answered.

I reasoned that after I finish writing today's events, there will be no other reason to remain here. I have been given instructions to go home and then go to Jerusalem.

When I returned to my writing rock to gather my final thoughts and make this last record of events, I noticed the level of ink in my jar. Until today the jar always had more than enough fluid, but now there is very little left. God has provided for me all my days, and especially these past 40 days. With the ink running low, I know that my task here is nearly completed.

Will God have another special task for me after I go to Jerusalem? I don't know. But he will provide for me, even if I am just to continue shepherding. Jesus said not even a sparrow is forgotten by God, and we are worth more than sparrows.[483] Thank you, God, for the privilege and honor you have given me to see your Son face to face.

I now make a most heartfelt request to whoever may eventually read these ramblings by a temporary author. Hopefully people will realize that what Daniel and I have seen and what I have written actually occurred; it wasn't a dream.

These scrolls record my firsthand report of 40 days with Jesus. People often tell stories they've heard from others; where the story originated, nobody knows. But this is not a passed-along story or a fabrication. This is a firsthand account. Please treat me as a friend, a trusted relation or a reliable neighbor, and then believe what I have written. I have spoken the truth and I can say, more than anyone else, God is my witness.

I understand that as time passes, it becomes hard to put your faith in something you haven't seen, but that is one of the reasons Jesus appeared for a while on this earth, and appeared to me also. When you have seen Jesus face to face, how can you deny his existence? How can you not believe?

My prayer is that you will believe, too. Put your faith in Jesus. He is real; he does exist.

Jesus is returning to his Father now, but he will return again as he promised.[484] We know God is faithful. The Scriptures are filled with his promises, and God does not lie.[485]

What should you do now? Believe in his Son and worship God! There is no other God. Show your love for all that He has done for you.[486]

While you wait for his return, look forward to eternal life with him. Jesus has conquered death—do not fear. This gift is free to all who believe.[487]

With tears of gratitude, I must record one final comment that Jesus made as he left us and walked towards the Golden Stairway, words that I will cherish all my remaining days until I, with my new body, see Him again. More comforting words were never spoken: "Remember, I am with you always, even to the end of the age."[488]

A New Beginning

Dr. Naveh set the papers down on the table, removed his glasses and wiped his eyes. Though he had already read Shemaiah's story, it still had a powerful effect on him. He looked across the table to see that his three guests, Anna, Ronia and Ilan, were wiping their eyes as well.

"There is a little more to this story," said Dr. Naveh, "an addendum if you please, but it is found in a different book. A man called Luke wrote this:"

> *After his suffering, he presented himself to them and gave many convincing proofs that he was alive. He appeared to them over a period of forty days and spoke about the kingdom of God.*

> *On one occasion, while he was eating with them, he gave them this command: "Do not leave Jerusalem, but wait for the gift my Father promised, which you have heard me speak about. For John baptized with water, but in a few days you will be baptized with the Holy Spirit."*[489]

> *...you will receive power when the Holy Spirit comes on you; and you will be my witnesses in Jerusalem, and in all Judea and Samaria, and to the ends of the earth."*

After he said this, he was taken up before their
very eyes, and a cloud hid him from their
sight. They were looking intently up into the
sky as he was going, when suddenly two men
dressed in white stood beside them. "Men of
Galilee," they said, "why do you stand here
looking into the sky? This same Jesus, who
has been taken from you into heaven, will
come back in the same way you have seen
him go into heaven." [490]

Ilan appeared the most moved by this reading. It took him a moment to gather his thoughts.

Finally he said, "I have been taught from the Tanakh since I was a little boy and I have always believed it. Occasionally, someone would ask me about this Jesus, called Christ, which the Christians talked about, but I always thought it was some story, like Greek mythology. I didn't believe it was true, but I must admit I was curious about this Jesus, because this topic has presented itself to me throughout my life. At times when my thoughts and activities would be occupied there would be a flash or a hint that there was someone or something I was neglecting; something more to my life that I was blocking, a path that I was avoiding, or a doorway that I was failing to go through.

"The verses of scripture that Shemaiah wrote out, I have also heard many times before. Like him, when the stories are connected together, I can see how they lead to…Can these stories about Jesus, the ones in the Christian Bible, be trusted as true?" Ilan asked.

It was at this point that Dr. Naveh interjected, "We have significant evidence about this Jesus. The writings and copies of writings in what Christians call the New Testament that have been found are very close to the time when Jesus lived on earth. From the perspective of one who has devoted his life to the study of ancient artifacts, the evidence is overwhelming.

"Let me explain a little about ancient documents. It has been determined that stories about someone exaggerate over time, not right away. Those stories that are written after 200 years begin to stretch. Consideration must then be given to how soon the original writings about someone were recorded. An original manuscript deteriorates, so the common practice then was to make copies. As copies are recovered they are compared for consistency. With people like Caesar, who lived before Christ, the earliest document was written 100 years after he died and the earliest copies, of which there are eight, were discovered 1,000 years after that. With Alexander the Great, who lived before Caesar, the earliest manuscript was written 400 years after his death and the first copy that is known to exist was 1,350 years after Alexander lived.

"As for Jesus, there are many who wrote about him. There were his followers, the first Christians. These records are very close to the actual time of Christ. When they were written, there were people living who could testify to their accuracy and dispute inaccuracies. They were written between 20 and 60 years after Jesus was crucified. As for copies of these documents, we are overwhelmed with copies, thousands of copies, whose consistency is impeccable, with the time span between copies and original being 20 and 400 years, depending on the author."

"Then you have writings that make it impossible to deny the existence of the ancient prophets, like the scrolls found at Qumran, the Dead Sea Scrolls. They are 1,000 years older than any scriptural manuscript previously found, and it's been determined that they were duplicated with greater than 99% accuracy. Amazing!

"Now, Shemaiah did introduce an interesting question regarding how the scrolls came to be along the Dead Sea at Qumran."

"Excuse me," said Ilan. "Why is that so important?"

"You must understand Ilan, nobody really knows how the scrolls got to Qumran. Let me explain the bigger picture," said Dr. Naveh. "So many of these pieces intertwine but you have to be careful with the religious evidence—we are still archaeologists—but each new discovery keeps building on previous ones. Certainly you've read in the Tanakh the writings of Daniel. Daniel even specified a time frame for the Anointed One that fits the lifetime of Jesus; earthly lifetime, that is."

Dr. Naveh then added: "Daniel also wrote verses that place the destruction of Jerusalem *after* the death of the Anointed One. Jerusalem *did* fall; that occurred in 68-70 A.D. It takes some time to explain Daniels time frame, and there is disagreement on this as well, but even the gospel writers recorded Jesus describing the destruction of Jerusalem. Now at the same time, we suddenly have all these fine scrolls appearing in Qumran. Did they come from the temple in Jerusalem? There are many theories but limited evidence.

"Now, that Joseph he mentioned, from Arimathea, was a unique person. Many stories surround him. He thought very highly of Jesus, and believed that he was God's Son. Remember, he placed Jesus in his own tomb. His contact with Jesus isn't doubted; it is recorded by all the gospel writers.[491] One story they alluded to, that is difficult to verify, is that he originally possessed the cup, or chalice, used by Jesus on the night before his crucifixion to serve wine to his disciples. You may have heard legends about the "Holy Grail." But I digress. Joseph's and Shemaiah's links to the scrolls will need further research. Very interesting."

Dr. Naveh took a sip from a plastic bottle of water before continuing.

"On top of that, there are also numerous writings by non-Christians, Hebrews and Romans, who recorded about Jesus as a matter of fact."

"Beyond the writings, we are always uncovering evidence through our work on our dig sites, by people such as Anna, which substantiates what is written. Like those artifacts, these scrolls will be analyzed. But I have no doubts. As the writings of Luke state, Jesus remained here for 40 days before ascending to Heaven. These scrolls tell us about some of Jesus' activities during those 40 days."

"So when you ask 'Can these stories in the Christian Bible about Jesus be true?', look at the evidence. Consider what you just heard me read—Shemaiah's own story—from the scrolls that you yourself uncovered."

Ilan then asked Dr. Naveh, "You are a Jew. Do you believe in this Jesus as the Son of God?"

A big smile filled Dr. Naveh's face. "Yes, I have for a long time. I might wear glasses but I'm not blind," he laughed. "But I also believe with my heart. I have confessed my sins to Jesus and I believe in his death and in his resurrection. His death paid the debt for my sinfulness in order to reconcile me with God, the Father, and I believe that he has filled me with his Holy Spirit. I certainly look forward to seeing him in Heaven when I leave this world."

Then Dr. Navel leaned forward toward Ilan and said, "But I cannot believe *for* you. Each person must believe for themselves. If you cannot believe this scroll, then believe the prophecies that were fulfilled through Jesus, the ones you were taught about. Or believe in the miracles that Jesus performed, or the many healings of illnesses and even from death that were testified about by so many. Believe in the way he died, just as Isaiah had foretold. Or believe in his resurrection from the dead and the many, many witnesses that saw him. Or believe in the testimony of his disciples, men who were themselves easily frightened, who scattered at the first sign of trouble when he was alive. But after they saw him die on the cross and then rise from the dead, they spent the rest of their lives telling everyone what they believed and what they had seen with their own eyes, even under threat of their own deaths, that Jesus is God's Anointed—the Savior."

Ilan saw the grand smile on Dr. Naveh's face. When he looked at his wife and daughter, he saw they were smiling as well. He asked them, "Ronia, do you believe? And you Anna, do you believe?"

Anna answered first.

"Daddy, I have believed for a long time. I couldn't deny the evidence that has been unearthed by so many archaeologists, or the many scrolls discovered and their consistency over a thousand years. I couldn't deny the spirit of God. Jesus lived, he died, and he is still alive. He *is* the one the prophets wrote about.

"I became a Christian, a believer, after I graduated, but I didn't want to create conflict between us so I have been praying, for many, many years, that something would happen, some sign or event would arise, that would open your eyes and your heart to Him. For ten years I have been praying. Mother knew, for I couldn't keep this joy to myself."

Ilan turned to Ronia, and asked, "Do you believe too?"

With tears rolling down her cheeks, she nodded her head in acknowledgment, and then embraced her husband for a few moments.

"We may be Jews," said Dr. Naveh, "but we believe in Jesus. We're completed Jews!"

Ilan then looked at his wife and daughter, and holding each one's hand, said, "I, too, now believe in Jesus as my Savior." He then bowed his head and said, "Jesus, please come into my life. I believe. Help increase my faith."[492]

References

[1] Exodus 34:29-30
[2] Matthew 9:2, Mark 2:5, Luke 5:20
[3] Matthew 3:2
[4] Luke 3:4
[5] Mark 10:46
[6] John 20:21
[7] Revelation 1:17
[8] Revelation 1:18
[9] Matthew 20:28, Mark 10:45
[10] Matthew 27:42
[11] John 19:30
[12] Hosea 6:2
[13] John 10:17
[14] John 10:18
[15] Matthew 16:17
[16] John 1:29
[17] Exodus 12:17
[18] John 16:24
[19] Jeremiah 29:11
[20] Isaiah 53:7
[21] Proverbs 3:5
[22] Proverbs 3:6
[23] 2 Timothy 3:16
[24] Isaiah 55:8-11
[25] Psalms 33:6
[26] John 1
[27] John 1:14
[28] Ezekiel 2:7

[29] Hebrews 4:12
[30] Luke 8:4-14
[31] Luke 8:16
[32] Isaiah 40:8
[33] Psalms 145:18, Psalms 119:151
[34] Psalms 119:147
[35] Luke 24:13-35
[36] Genesis 3:15
[37] Genesis 12:3
[38] Genesis 17:19
[39] Genesis 22:8
[40] 1Co 10:13
[41] Exodus 12:12
[42] Deuteronomy 18:15
[43] 2 Samuel 7:12
[44] 2 Samuel 7:13-14
[45] Psalms 2, Psalms 110:1, Matthew 26:64
[46] Isaiah 7:14
[47] Isaiah 9:6
[48] Micah 5:2
[49] Isaiah 9:1
[50] James 1:10
[51] Psalm 135:14
[52] John 20:28
[53] Matthew 6:25
[54] John 1:45
[55] John 1:49
[56] John 1:51
[57] Matthew 20:19
[58] John 16:16
[59] John 11:1-44
[60] Luke 8:40-56
[61] Luke 7:12-15
[62] Matthew 28:7
[63] Matthew 26:32, Mark 14:28
[64] John 20:6,7
[65] Luke 24:34

[66] Luke 24:36
[67] John 20:22
[68] John 21:3
[69] John 1:47
[70] Matthew 26:32
[71] Matthew 28:10
[72] Luke 24:33
[73] Samuel I 16:7
[74] 2 Corinthians 12:9
[75] John 16:7
[76] Matthew 24:9
[77] John 16:8-11
[78] John 14:26
[79] John 15:26-27
[80] Acts 1:4
[81] Luke 24:47
[82] John 15:20
[83] Matthew 23:34
[84] Acts 1:20
[85] John 21:18
[86] Acts 7
[87] Acts 9:16
[88] John 7:5
[89] 1 Corinthians 15:7
[90] Matthew 10:33, Luke 11:49
[91] Matthew 10:28
[92] Philippians 1:21
[93] Romans 5:8
[94] John 13:35
[95] Acts 9:36-43, Acts 20:9-11
[96] Acts 7:56
[97] Acts 2:4-6
[98] Luke 18:17
[99] Psalms 127:3
[100] Genesis 1:22
[101] Heb 5:12-14
[102] Psalms 10:4

[103] Isaiah 2:12
[104] Ephesians 2:1
[105] John 12:30
[106] 1 Colossians 15:22
[107] Exodus 20:1-11
[108] Mt 22:37, Exodus 20:1
[109] Jeremiah 10:10, Mark 8:33, Matthew 4:10
[110] Psalms 37:16-17
[111] Luke 12:13
[112] Isaiah 47:8-11
[113] 1 Timothy 6:10
[114] Matthew 6:33
[115] Matthew 6:24
[116] 1 Corinthians 8:6, Hag 2:8-9
[117] Matthew 6:32
[118] Haggai 2:8
[119] Psalms 50:10
[120] Matthew 22:39-40
[121] Deuteronomy 11:13-17
[122] Jonah 3:5-10, Mt 12:41
[123] Nahum 1:1 – 3:19
[124] Nahum 1:2
[125] Jeremiah 10:10
[126] Ezekiel 28:4-10
[127] Daniel 4:3, 2 Peter 1:11
[128] 1 Kings 9:4, 1Kings 14:8
[129] 1 Samuel 8:7-8
[130] 1 Samuel 8:10-22
[131] Deuteronomy 15:1-6
[132] Proverbs 22:7
[133] Deuteronomy 15:7-11
[134] Malachi 3:10
[135] Deuteronomy 28:13
[136] Isaiah 9:6
[137] Matthew 5:10, Acts 8:1
[138] Luke 4:5-8, Deuteronomy 6:13
[139] Judges 8:23

[140] 2 Chronicles 7:14
[141] Deuteronomy 28:1
[142] Deuteronomy 28:2-14
[143] Matthew 23:12
[144] John 1:12
[145] Matthew 18:4
[146] John 14:1
[147] 2 Samuel 6:14
[148] Psalm 73
[149] Genesis 1:22
[150] Genesis 30:1
[151] Psalms 127:3-5
[152] Ezekiel 16:21
[153] Leviticus 18:21, Proverbs 6:17; Isaiah 1:15; Jeremiah 22:17
[154] Psalms 139:13, Psalms 139:15-16
[155] Jeremiah 1:5
[156] Matthew 18:10
[157] Matthew 18:14
[158] Mark 3:28
[159] John 1:12
[160] Deuteronomy 11:19
[161] Deuteronomy 11:19
[162] Isaiah 2:3
[163] Proverbs 20:11, Pr 22:15, Pr 23:13, Pr 29:15, Heb 12:10
[164] Deuteronomy 8:5, Proverbs 3:12, 1 Cor. 11:32, Heb 12:5,6, Revelation 3:19
[165] Isaiah 7:14, Matthew 1:23
[166] Genesis 1:28
[167] Jeremiah 29:11
[168] Luke 9:48
[169] Philippians 2:10, Isaiah 45:23, Matthew 28:18
[170] Genesis 12:3, Psalms 72:17, Luke 1:48
[171] Isaiah 52:13 - 53:12
[172] Daniel 9:26
[173] Zechariah 12:10
[174] Psalms 22:16

[175] Psalms 22:18
[176] Matthew 27:35
[177] Psalms 22:7-8
[178] Psalms 22:17
[179] Psalms 22:1
[180] Psalms 34:20
[181] Amos 8:9
[182] John 21:11
[183] Matthew 26:35
[184] Matthew 26:69-74
[185] Matthew 26:34
[186] Matthew 11:28-30
[187] Matthew 9:6
[188] Matthew 18:21
[189] Matthew 16:18
[190] Luke 7:47
[191] Revelation 3:20
[192] Luke 24:47
[193] Psalms 56:11, John 12:36, Deuteronomy 33:27
[194] John 6:9
[195] John 1:48
[196] Luke 1:37, Luke 18:27, Matthew 19:26, Mark 10:27
[197] Matthew 14:19-20
[198] Exodus 16:13
[199] Exodus 12:37
[200] Exodus 16:35
[201] 1 Kings 17:4-6
[202] 1 Kings 17:4-6
[203] Kings I 17:14-16
[204] Genesis 21:14-19
[205] Psalms 65:9
[206] Job 38:29-33
[207] Matthew 6:26
[208] Matthew 6:25-33
[209] Psalms 95:7
[210] Deuteronomy 30:16
[211] Mark 9:43

[212] Deuteronomy 8:19
[213] Ps 14:3
[214] Matthew 5:17
[215] Matthew 5:18
[216] Psalm 139:7-11
[217] John 3:16
[218] Deuteronomy 31:6, 2 Timothy 2:11-13
[219] Psalm 147:10-11, Psalm51:17
[220] Luke 7:37-50, John 8:11, Luke 19:5, Luke 19:8-9
[221] Ezekiel 33:11, 2 Peter 3:9, 1Titus2:4
[222] 1 John 3:8
[223] Isaiah 61:1
[224] John 3:16
[225] 1 John 1:8
[226] James 1:5
[227] 2 Corinthians 1:3
[228] John 14:27
[229] Genesis 3:24
[230] Genesis 3:19
[231] Genesis 3:15
[232] Genesis 6:5
[233] Genesis 6:9
[234] 1Ki 19:18
[235] Genesis 6:9, Leviticus 26:12, Deuteronomy 10:12, Joshua 22:5, Kings I 2:3, Isaiah 2:3, Jeremiah 7:23
[236] 1 Thessalonians 5:9
[237] Matthew 11:28-30
[238] Joshua 1:13, Psalm 62:1, 5
[239] Matthew 6:25-34
[240] Mark 11:22
[241] Psalms 127:2
[242] Matthew 11:28
[243] Philippians 4:6
[244] Matthew 17:20
[245] Mark 11:24
[246] Luke 11:8, Luke 18:1
[247] Mark 11:25

---

[248] Jeremiah 29:12
[249] James 4:3-10
[250] John 16:7
[251] Romans 8:6
[252] Matthew6:9-15
[253] Matthew 6:7-8
[254] 1 Thessalonians 5:16-18
[255] Proverbs 3:5-6
[256] Luke 12:15-21
[257] James 1:5
[258] Psalms 94:19
[259] John 14:27
[260] 2 Chronicles 1:11-12
[261] John 14:13
[262] John 14:23
[263] James 4:3
[264] John 14:12
[265] John 14:13
[266] John 16:33
[267] 1 Samuel 16:7
[268] Genesis 6:9
[269] Psalms 37:7, Psalms 38:15, Psalms 39:7, Psalms 17:5-6
[270] 2 Corinthians 4:18
[271] John 16:33
[272] Psalms 39:6
[273] Matthew 6:10
[274] Psalms 27:14
[275] Psalms 27:8
[276] Psalms 37:7
[277] Psalms 1:1-3
[278] John 8:12, Psalms 119:105
[279] Romans 12:1
[280] Psalms 139:13
[281] Proverbs 5:21
[282] Psalm 57:2, Proverbs 19:21, Isaiah 46:8-13
[283] Luke 8:15
[284] Esther 4:14

[285] 1 Timothy 6:6-7
[286] Proverbs 3:5-6
[287] Psalm 103:20-22
[288] Luke 9:29
[289] Revelation 4:6
[290] Matthew 14:25-27
[291] John 20:26, Luke 24:36
[292] John 8:12
[293] Matthew5:13-16
[294] Matthew 28:19
[295] Romans 10:13-15
[296] Exodus 34:30
[297] Matthew 27:51
[298] Matthew 18:20
[299] John 4:24
[300] Hebrews 10:25
[301] Revelation 21:3
[302] Genesis 2:16-17
[303] Genesis 3:19
[304] Hebrews 9:27
[305] Luke 22:42-44
[306] Luke 1:78-79
[307] Isaiah 9:2
[308] Jeremiah 29:11
[309] Proverbs 11:19
[310] Leviticus 20
[311] Psalms 55:15
[312] Psalms 55:4
[313] Psalms 23:4
[314] Luke 1:79
[315] John 14:1
[316] John 5:24
[317] Psalms 139:24
[318] Psalms 39:12
[319] John 12:25
[320] Matthew 5:12
[321] Matthew 10:28

322 Luke 18:27
323 John 3:16
324 Gen 3:19
325 Genesis 1:27
326 John 4:24
327 Ecclesiastes 12:7
328 Luke 8:55
329 Luke 23:46
330 Matthew 13:15
331 John 10:18
332 Matthew 27:60
333 Psalm 16:10
334 Luke 23:43
335 2 Peter 2:4
336 Luke 16:19-31
337 John 5:24
338 John 5:29, Matthew 25:46
339 John 5:28-29
340 Isaiah 26:19
341 1 Corinthians 15:42-44
342 2 Corinthians 5:8
343 Acts 17:26, Ephesians 2:10
344 Psalms 32:8
345 John 4:23
346 John 5:24
347 2 Peter 3:9
348 Matthew 7:13-14
349 Matthew 24:36
350 Matthew 24:44
351 John 16:33
352 John 14:1
353 Hosea 13:14
354 John 16:33
355 Matthew 14:12-13
356 2 Corinthians 1:3
357 Psalms 116:15
358 2 Corinthians 1:4

[359] Ecclesiastes 3:11
[360] Isaiah 64:4
[361] 1 Corinthians 2:9
[362] Luke 22:42
[363] John 14:2-3
[364] 1 Chronicles16:27
[365] Revelation 21:2-3
[366] Revelation 21:20-21
[367] John 14:2
[368] Genesis 1:1, Genesis 2:1
[369] 1 Corinthians 15:42-44
[370] Isaiah 65:17, Isaiah 66:22, 2 Peter 3:13, Revelation 21:1
[371] Ephesians 6:12, Job 1:6
[372] Revelation 12:9
[373] Matthew 24:35
[374] Isaiah 65:17
[375] Jeremiah 31:34
[376] Revelation 22:15
[377] Revelation 21:8
[378] Revelation 21:1
[379] Revelation 15 - 16
[380] Revelation 21:3-4
[381] 1 Peter 5:10
[382] Psalms 16:11
[383] Psalms 23:6
[384] Psalms 61:4
[385] Revelation 5:13
[386] 1 Thessalonians 4:14, John 5:24
[387] 2 Peter 1:11
[388] Revelation 5:11
[389] Revelation 7:9-10
[390] Revelation 11:18
[391] Romans 15:4
[392] Isaiah 55:11
[393] Revelation 11:18, Matthew 16:27, Matthew 5:46, Matthew 6:1,   Matthew 10:41, Ephesians 6:8, Revelation 22:12

[394] John 5:17
[395] Genesis 2:15
[396] Genesis 2:16-17
[397] Revelation 22:3
[398] Ephesians 2:6
[399] John 14:1, John 14:27
[400] Matthew 11:30
[401] Ephesians 6:8
[402] Matthew 11:28
[403] Revelation 14:13
[404] Revelation 14:11
[405] Revelation 21:21
[406] Revelation 22:1-2
[407] Matthew 24:36
[408] John 14:2
[409] Numbers 23:19
[410] Matthew 13:17
[411] Revelation 21:3
[412] Matthew 14:21, Matthew 15:38, Luke 12:1
[413] 1 Corinthians 15:6
[414] Exodus 3:2-4
[415] Exodus 33:9
[416] Deuteronomy 4:12, Deuteronomy 5:4
[417] Exodus 24:9-11
[418] Numbers 12:7-8
[419] Deuteronomy 34:10
[420] 1 Kings 19:12
[421] Luke 10:24
[422] Ephesians 2:8-9
[423] Psalm 63
[424] 1 Peter 1:10-12
[425] Heb. 11:13-16
[426] Psalm 112:1
[427] Leviticus 16:2
[428] Hebrews 9:4
[429] 1 Samuel 6:19, 2 Samuel 6:7
[430] Colossians 1:16

[431] Genesis 1:1
[432] Isaiah 40:26
[433] Isaiah 42:5
[434] Genesis 1:21
[435] Genesis 1:24
[436] Genesis 1:27
[437] Psalm 147:11
[438] Psalm 111:10
[439] Mark 1:4
[440] Matthew 28:19
[441] Hebrews 11
[442] 1 Corinthians 13:13
[443] 1 John 4:7, 1 John 3:1
[444] 1 John 4:9, John 3:16
[445] Romans 5:8
[446] 1 John 4:10
[447] 1 Thessalonians 3:12
[448] John 1:12
[449] John 13:34
[450] Nahum 1:7, John 10:13-15, Ephesians 5:29, 1 Peter 5:7, Hebrews 13:5, Deuteronomy 31:6
[451] James 4:8
[452] 1 John 5:9-12
[453] Matthew 20:25
[454] John 13:15
[455] Matthew 20:28
[456] John 13:1-17
[457] Mark 1:15
[458] Psalms 149:4, Matthew 5:5
[459] Titus 3:4-8
[460] Matthew 5:3
[461] Matthew 5:4
[462] Matthew 5:6, John 15:15
[463] John14:13-14
[464] Matthew 6:3-4
[465] Luke 4:8
[466] Proverbs 10:12, 1 Peter 4:8, 1 Corinthians 13:4

[467] John 15:20
[468] Matthew 5:10-12
[469] Luke 12:12
[470] Romans 12:2
[471] Romans 15:4, 2 Timothy 3:16
[472] John 20:29
[473] Luke 19:41-44
[474] Luke 23:50
[475] Isaiah 55:11
[476] Matthew 11:30
[477] Acts 1:12
[478] Psalm 110:1
[479] Revelation 21:6 & 22:13
[480] John 16:7
[481] John 14:2
[482] Acts 1:11
[483] Luke 12:6-7
[484] Revelation 22:7, 12, 20
[485] Numbers 23:19
[486] Revelation 22: 9
[487] Revelation 22:17
[488] Matthew 28:20
[489] Acts 1:3-5 (NLT)
[490] Acts 1:8-11 (NLT)
[491] Matthew 27:57, Mark 15:43, Luke 23:51, John 19:3
[492] Mark 9:24

Also from
Cardamom Publishers

Women of the Old Testament:
14 In-Depth Bible Studies for Teens
with Mother-Daughter Discussion Starters

By Barbara Frank

This curriculum is designed to teach teens about Old Testament women while helping them relate these famous women's stories to their own and their mothers' lives.

Designed for grades 8-12 and up, this book is arranged in an assignment format, and can be completed in one school year of daily work. The answer key is included for ease of correcting, with specific Bible references for every answer.

ISBN: 978-0-9742181-5-1, 306 pages

"I really like the format of this Bible curriculum,
and think the chance to study some great female
role models is good for your maturing teen girls.
... I don't have any daughters, but if I did I would
have loved to do this study. I'm sure any young
woman will grow in grace and knowledge as she
works through these meaningful Bible studies."
Kathy Davis
homeschoolbuzz.com

For more information go to:
www.CardamomPublishers.com